Party Time

Have you been invited to all these sleepovers?

Party Time

Fiona Cummings

HarperCollins *Children's Books*

The Sleepover Club ® is a registered trademark
of HarperCollins*Publishers* Ltd

First published in Great Britain as *Happy New Year Sleepover Club*
by HarperCollins *Children's Books* in 1999
This edition published by HarperCollins *Children's Books* in 2009
HarperCollins *Children's Books* is a division of HarperCollins*Publishers* Ltd,
77-85 Fulham Palace Road, Hammersmith, London W6 8JB

www.harpercollins.co.uk

2

Text copyright © Fiona Cummings 1999

Original series characters, plotlines and settings © Rose Impey 1997

The author asserts the moral right to be
identified as the author of this work.

ISBN-13 978-0-00-730994-8

Printed and bound in England by
Clays Ltd, St Ives plc

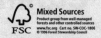

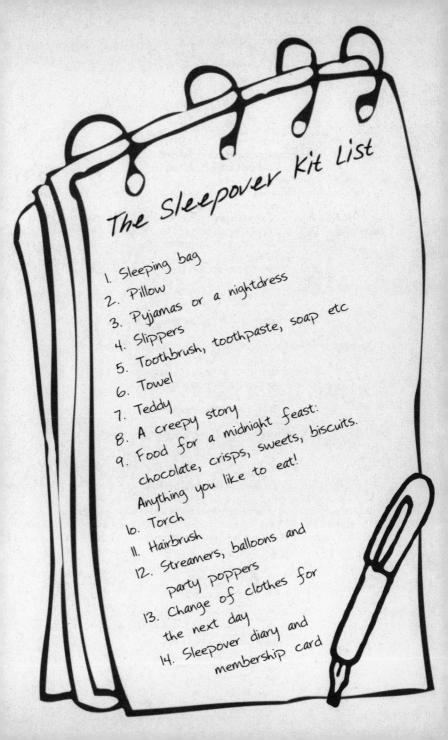

The Sleepover Kit List

1. Sleeping bag
2. Pillow
3. Pyjamas or a nightdress
4. Slippers
5. Toothbrush, toothpaste, soap etc
6. Towel
7. Teddy
8. A creepy story
9. Food for a midnight feast:
   chocolate, crisps, sweets, biscuits.
   Anything you like to eat!
10. Torch
11. Hairbrush
12. Streamers, balloons and
    party poppers
13. Change of clothes for
    the next day
14. Sleepover diary and
    membership card

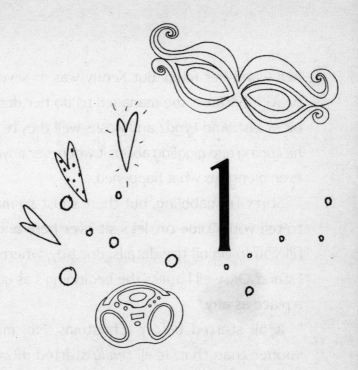

1

Hi there. I know what you're going to say. "Frankie, you're late!"

I'm right aren't I? That's what the others are always saying these days. It always used to be Lyndz who was late, and I was super-dooper organised. Not any more! My house is so manic at the moment it's a wonder I ever get out at all. But I'll tell you all about that in a minute. We really ought to sit down and catch up on all the goss. Poor Fliss is still recovering. It all got a bit much for her – and her mum. But Kenny was in seventh heaven because she managed to do her doctor bit at last. And Lyndz and Rosie, well they're still hiccuping and giggling about it whenever anyone even mentions what happened.

Sorry I'm gabbling, but there's just so much to tell you. Come on, let's sit over here and I'll fill you in on all the details. But boy, where do I start? OK, well I guess the beginning's as good a place as any.

It all started before Christmas. No, much sooner than that. It all *really* started months ago when I found out that Mum was pregnant. I'd wanted a little baby brother or sister for as long as I could remember, and when I found out that Mum was expecting a baby I was totally blown away by the excitement. The others all tried their hardest to put me off by giving me loads of grisly details.

"Babies are just totally embarrassing," warned Lyndz. "Didn't you learn *anything* when we were helping Rosie's sister with her babysitting last time?" (Now that's a story and a half – if you haven't read about it yet, you're in for a real treat!) "Babies are either pooing or being sick. And my older brothers aren't much better."

Poor Lyndz has *four* brothers and she reckons that they make her life a misery.

"At least you'll be a lot older than your brother or sister," reasoned Kenny. "You'll be able to boss it about all the time. How cool is that!"

Her eyes gleamed at the thought. Molly the Monster, as you know, is only a year older than Kenny, but is one major super-witch when it comes to being horrible.

"Yeah, when you're wanting to go out, it'll be pestering you to play!" laughed Rosie. "Tiff always says that I'm a major pain when she's getting glammed up, and she's only four years older than me! But I'm sure that you'll have a lot more patience than her," she added. "And you won't have a boyfriend as ugly as Spud either."

The others all nodded.

"I won't have a boyfriend at all!" I said indignantly.

9

"Yes you will!" snorted Fliss. "When the baby is our age, you'll be twenty! Imagine that. You'll probably be at university then. You might even be married!"

We all guffawed.

"No way!" I yelled. "You'll be married to Ryan Scott, more like!"

Fliss just blushed and went all giggly – as usual!

We had loads of conversations like that, and the others always told me horror stories about being a sister. Now don't get me wrong. I was still desperate to have a baby to look after, but the more they told me, the more nervous I got. I mean, it just seemed so long since I'd found out about the baby, and it wasn't even due until January.

"I wish it would hurry up!" I told Mum one day at the beginning of December. "I just want to get on with being a big sister."

"Well, I'm not ready to be a new mum again just yet, thank you very much!" she laughed. "We've still got far too much to do!"

That was true. They still hadn't sorted out

where the baby was going to sleep for one thing. At this rate, it would be sharing Pepsi's basket in the kitchen!

"But how will I know if I'll be any good as a sister?" I asked Mum.

"You'll be just great!" she smiled, ruffling my hair. "If you're so worried, you could always practise on something. There are some schools that make students look after a bag of flour as though it's a baby. I know it sounds weird, but it gets them used to having someone else to think about."

"You want me to push a bag of flour about in a pram?" I asked, open-mouthed.

"It doesn't have to be a bag of flour," Mum explained. "You could use one of your old dolls. The important thing is to treat it as though it really is a baby. No dumping it under your bed when you're fed up with it. Just look after it for a day or so and I guarantee it will open your eyes."

Yes, I know, I know – it sounds really wacky, doesn't it? But I thought it might be worth a try. I went up to my room and pulled the box of old dolls out of my cupboard. I hadn't looked at them for absolutely *ages* and it felt really weird holding them again.

"You're way too old for all this, Frankie," I told myself.

But I got them all out anyway and sat them in a line on my bed. I felt kind of funny seeing them like that, because it brought back memories of when I was little. I had this one doll I used to call Diz that I used to take everywhere with me. I picked it up now, and it looked so tiny and shabby. I felt really bad, like I'd abandoned it or something. But I couldn't use that as my baby because it just didn't look right. It was too small for a start and had matted wool hair. The others didn't look much better, to be honest with you.

Then I spotted 'the doll with no name'. A friend of Mum's had given it to me just as I was growing out of my doll phase and I'd never really played with it. But it was about the right size for a baby. It had no hair and it still smelt kind of clean and new.

"Come on then!" I said, picking her up. "You can be my baby. Are you going to be a good girl?" I cooed, tickling her under the chin.

I was amazed how quickly I got into all the baby stuff. Before long it didn't seem weird at all to be wandering round with a doll. But you know my friends. As soon as they saw me with the doll one Saturday, they thought I'd lost it completely.

"Francesca Thomas, have you gone mad?" screeched Kenny when she saw me carrying Izzy. (I called my doll Isobel, Izzy for short, because that's what I wanted Mum to call the baby if she had a girl.)

"I'm just winding her after her feed!" I explained, patting Izzy's back.

"I'll wind you in a minute!" she yelled. "What are you like?"

No amount of explaining what I was doing

13

would make her shut up. And the others weren't much better. Even Fliss had a go at me.

"You look really silly, Frankie," she hissed. "I wish you'd put that stupid doll down. It's going to be really embarrassing if anyone sees us."

I must admit that I did feel a bit of a loon taking it to the shops with us, but a deal is a deal. Mum said that I had to treat the doll just like a real baby. If I had to go to the shops then it would just have to come with me. I couldn't leave Izzy at home, could I?

"Couldn't you ask your mum to babysit?" asked Lyndz. Kenny rolled her eyes.

"I don't think so. I'm supposed to be learning how to be a big sister," I explained. "Mum already knows how to be a mum, so asking her to babysit a doll would be a bit pointless."

"The whole thing's pointless if you ask me," grumbled Kenny. "Well, are we going to the shops or not?"

To start with, I made a sort of sling with my scarf and kept Izzy snuggled under my jacket. The

14

December wind was pretty fierce and I didn't want her to get cold.

"You are sad, sad, sad," chanted Kenny, as I kept fussing beneath my jacket.

"At least no one can see the doll," said Fliss. "You just look fat!"

"Thanks very much!" I said, feeling a bit miffed.

But it soon got uncomfortable having Izzy in one position so I started wriggling and jiggling, trying to move her about. It didn't help that her arms and legs weren't all squidgy like a real baby's. They were rigid plastic and kept digging into me.

"Don't do that, Frankie!" Rosie reprimanded me. "You look as though you've got ants in your pants or something. People are looking at you."

It was true. There were hundreds of people about doing their Christmas shopping, and I could sense that most of them were glancing at me and frowning.

"Maybe I should just show them Izzy," I suggested, unzipping my jacket.

"Don't do that!" the others all yelled together.

"That would be a major embarrassment for all of us," hissed Kenny.

"Hey, what's that poster?" Fliss suddenly shouted at the top of her voice. She was being so OTT, it was obvious that she was trying to divert our attention. She sort of galloped over to the noticeboard at the end of the high street. The rest of us cracked up and galloped after her. It wasn't easy with a doll poking you in the chest with every step, I can tell you.

"It's advertising a New Year's Eve party at the church hall," explained Fliss, standing in front of the poster. "Do you think we'll be able to go?"

"Not a chance," said Rosie. "My mum's only ever let me stay up to see the New Year in once, and that was because I was sick."

"I'm not sure I'd want to go anyway," Kenny said. "It'll be full of boring old duffers who we don't even know. It'd be much better to have a New Year's Eve party of our own."

"Yes!" we all screamed. "Why don't we? It'd be so cool!"

16

"We should try to organise a special New Year's Eve sleepover," I suggested. "I mean, we're usually awake till well past midnight when we're together anyway. It would be great to stay up properly. Everyone else'll be up too, so who could object?"

We were so excited we started doing a little dance together on the pavement. And that's when Izzy fell out of my jacket and bounced on to the ground.

"Oh no!" I screamed, picking her up. "I've killed her!"

"Erm, earth to Frankie!" hooted Kenny. "It is only a doll, you know!"

"But it's supposed to be my baby sister," I spluttered. "What if I do that to her?"

"Don't be crazy!" shrieked Lyndz. "Do you think your parents would really let us loose in charge of their baby? I don't think so!"

"But even so," I wailed. "I was supposed to take care of Izzy and I haven't. I'm going to be a useless sister!"

Fliss led me over to a nearby bench and we all sat down.

"You're going to be a great sister, Frankie," she reassured me. "That was just an accident when you forgot about the d… I mean, Izzy."

"But what if I forget about the real baby when I'm supposed to be looking after it?" I asked.

"Believe me, you *never* forget when you've got a baby around," Lyndz grinned. "They never stop crying. And they usually smell disgusting too!"

I was rocking Izzy in my arms and the others were all bending over her, just like she was real.

"Well I've seen everything now!" boomed a loud voice.

We looked up quickly, but with sinking hearts we already knew who it was. Why had the M&Ms picked that exact minute to walk past us?

"Aw, has Francesca got a baby? Diddums," said Emma Hughes in a stupid voice.

"Does she like playing with her dolly then?"

cooed Emma's sidekick Emily Berryman.

"I always knew you were a big baby, Thomas!" cackled Emma. "I grew out of dolls when I was about four. You lot have never grown up, have you?"

Kenny was seething, I could sense it.

"Frankie's taking part in some scientific research, if you must know," she said in her weariest voice. "Not that you'd understand."

"Oh right, that's the first time I've heard playing with dolls called 'scientific research'," sneered Emily. "Why don't you face it? You're a load of little kids!"

They both screamed with laughter and tottered down the high street on their platform wedges.

"I don't believe that!" Fliss had her head in her hands. "Of all the people to see us with that stupid doll!"

"They'll never let us forget it," moaned Rosie. "It'll be all round the school on Monday!"

"Not if I've got anything to do with it," fumed Kenny through gritted teeth.

And when Kenny spoke like that the rest of us knew that it meant trouble. Trouble with a capital T!

2

To be honest with you, seeing those two galumphing gorillas put a real damper on our whole weekend. We didn't even discuss the New Year sleepover again, so you can tell how bad we were feeling. And Kenny went totally weird. I mean, even weirder than usual. When the rest of us were panicking about the M&Ms, she was like, lost in a trance. Then she suddenly leapt up and announced that she had to go to the shop to buy some – get this –

JELLY CUBES. I mean, here we were, facing doom and disaster from our biggest rivals, and Kenny's planning a party tea! But she just had this crazy look on her face and kept saying that she needed jelly cubes to make everything all right. I prefer chocolate to cheer myself up actually, but each to their own, as my gran always says.

Anyway, before we said goodbye to each other on Saturday, we arranged to meet outside school on Monday morning. That way we could all face the Gruesome Twosome together.

I had a really bad feeling as I walked to school that morning. Doom and panic whizzed about in my stomach like one of Kenny's disastrous cooking experiments. Fliss and Rosie were already standing together by the wall, and they looked as green as I felt. Only Lyndz seemed as bright and breezy as usual. I swear that if that girl was any more laid back, she'd be permanently asleep!

"Oh come on, we've taken flak from the

M&Ms before," she reasoned. "How bad can it be this time?"

Nobody answered.

When we got to the gate we could see the M&Ms in a little huddle with their stupid mate Alana 'Banana' Palmer.

"I wonder where Kenny is? She ought to be here by now," mumbled Fliss. Her teeth were chattering, and I don't think it was because of the cold.

Rosie stuck her tongue out and pulled gruesome faces at the M&Ms – well, at their backs, to be precise. Then she mumbled something no one could understand.

"What?"

Rosie stopped pulling faces. "I said 'I don't know but she seemed really mad on Saturday'!" she explained.

Just before the whistle went, Kenny came flying up to us, holding tightly on to her school bag. She didn't look mad now. In fact, she looked positively perky.

23

"What's up with you?" I asked her suspiciously.

"You'll see," she grinned. "Just distract the M&Ms for a couple of minutes when we get inside."

"What?" Fliss looked horrified. "But we're trying to stay out of their way!"

"We can't avoid them for ever," Kenny told her calmly. "Better to get all their sarky comments over with at once."

Now it wasn't like her to be so rational, so I knew she had something majorly wicked up her sleeve.

Just then the whistle sounded, so we had no choice but to go into school.

"Remember – distract them!" hissed Kenny as we headed towards the classroom.

As it was December, we were all muffled up in coats and scarves, so we knew that we'd be in the cloakroom with the M&Ms for a few minutes. When we got there, Kenny gave me this big wink, and headed behind the coat rack. The M&Ms were already tugging off their boots. As soon as they saw us they started laughing in a really OTT way.

24

"Have you got your doll under there then, Frankie?" asked Emma loudly so that everyone could hear.

"We were wondering if you'd like to start a little dolly crèche in the corner of the classroom," Emily Berryman rasped in her gruff voice.

"Or better still, go back to the nursery class!" guffawed Emma. "Four-year-olds are about on your level, aren't they?"

We just took off our coats and ignored them. I could see Kenny ferreting about in the M&Ms' bags and there was a bit of a weird smell, but I couldn't tell what she was doing. All I did know was that when the M&Ms looked ready to go into the classroom, I had to stall them.

"I was conducting an experiment, that's all!" I blurted out. The others looked horrified.

"You make me laugh Thomas, you really do!" sniffed Emma.

"What kind of experiment?" asked Emily curiously.

I didn't really want to tell them about Mum

being pregnant and everything. It felt like if they knew, they'd make fun of that too and it would spoil everything.

As I was trying to think of an answer, Kenny appeared and said, "She's not going to tell you is she? It's classified information."

"Get real!" snapped Emma, and gathering up their bags, they walked into the classroom.

"What were you doing?" I asked Kenny when they'd gone.

"You'll find out soon enough!" she smiled, and tapped her nose.

At least Mrs Weaver had something exciting to take our mind off the dreadful duo. At the end of the Christmas term, each class performs in a concert. This year Mrs Weaver told us that we would be writing our own play.

"Well it's not a play exactly," she explained. "It's going to be a series of sketches about the twentieth century."

We all looked pretty blank.

"Say someone born in 1900 was still alive,"

Mrs Weaver continued. "What changes would they have seen?"

"There's more football on the telly now!" Ryan Scott shouted out.

Mrs Weaver flashed him one of her 'you-think-you've-got-the-better-of-me-but-you-haven't-really' smiles.

"I think what you mean, Ryan, is that yes, we do have television now. But there wasn't a broadcasting service at all until 1936."

"Imagine life without *Match of the Day*!" moaned Danny McCloud. "Bummer!"

"That's exactly what I want you to do, Danny! Imagine what life would be like," Mrs Weaver went on. "I want you to think of all the things you take for granted now, and find out when they were invented and how they have developed. Work in your groups, but I don't want any noise. Understood?"

We all nodded, and started chattering away.

"I love doing this kind of thing," I told the others. "You learn about stuff without even realising it."

But Kenny wasn't listening. She was propped up on the desk, eyeballing the M&Ms. "Open your bags," she was muttering under her breath. "Come on!"

"There's almost too much to think about," Lyndz said, doodling on her notebook. "I mean, *loads* of stuff must have happened since 1900."

"Yeah, but what's the most important?" I asked. I looked around the classroom. "I mean, look at computers. They haven't been around for that long, have they? And now everyone's got them."

"And they use them in supermarkets and banks and stuff where you can't even see them," added Rosie.

"My gran thinks supermarkets are really new!" laughed Lyndz. "She says that she used to have to queue up at loads of different shops for her shopping. Imagine that – it would take *ages*!"

Fliss didn't seem to be listening to the rest of us either. She was doing loads of little drawings. Typical Fliss.

"Come on Fliss, we're supposed to be working!" I told her.

"I *am* working!" she snapped, showing me her drawings of fashion designs. "Clothes have changed loads since 1900. Women still wore long dresses then. And Mum said that when girls started wearing mini-skirts in the 1960s, it caused a real stir. There must have been loads of changes in between."

Fliss did have a point.

"Drawing dollies, are we?" Emma Hughes sidled across and peered over Fliss's shoulder.

"No I'm not!" snapped Fliss, and covered her work with her arm.

"What are you doing, Thomas? The development of experiments using dolls?" asked Emily Berryman.

They both giggled in that stupid way they have.

"And what are *you* doing? The history of not doing any work, as usual," Kenny sneered. "You haven't even got anything out of your bags yet."

"We're just going to look at some books!" Emma 'the Queen' Hughes said crossly, and they both stalked past us to the book corner.

29

We settled down again and made loads of lists. Nearly everything we could think of that was important in our lives had been invented since 1900. We looked things up in books and on the computer, and the time flashed past. We even talked about the work over break too, which is very unusual for us. Well, the rest of us talked about it – Kenny didn't. She kept trying to see whether the M&Ms had their bags with them. They didn't.

When we got back into the classroom after break, Mrs Weaver said that she wanted some idea of what we would all be contributing to our play. I could see the M&Ms huddled together with their cronies. They kept flashing looks over to our table, then whispering and giggling together.

"Well, what are we going to do?" I asked the others. "Any ideas?"

"Fashion!" Fliss piped up. "Please let's! It'd be dead cool."

"I don't want to get involved in a stupid fashion show!" grumbled Kenny.

30

"It won't be a fashion show, it's history. Please, pretty please!" Fliss pleaded.

The rest of us looked at each other.

"Oh all right!" we agreed, but Kenny looked pretty disgusted.

"Right then, who's going to start?" asked Mrs Weaver.

Emma Hughes stuck up her hand and started waving it about. She always has to get noticed. And with Mrs Weaver, it usually works.

"Yes, Emma, what have you got planned?"

"Well, we thought we'd trace the history of fashion since 1900," she said, ever so sweetly.

"But that's what *we* were going to do!" squealed Fliss. "That's not fair, she's copied us!"

Poor Fliss was quite red in the face and angry.

"Now, Felicity, there are lots of exciting ideas to cover," soothed Mrs Weaver. "I'll give your group a few more minutes to think of another topic. Well done, Emma, that's a splendid idea."

I thought Fliss was going to cry, I really did. Especially when we turned round and saw

31

the stupid M&Ms and their awful cronies grinning at us.

"We'll get you!" Kenny mouthed to them menacingly.

"What should we do?" I whispered to the others.

"What about television and radio – stuff like that?" suggested Rosie.

But just then Ryan Scott announced that they were covering television.

"I don't believe it!" grumbled Rosie.

"What about computers, then?" I suggested.

"OK!" the others agreed, but you could tell that they weren't very enthusiastic.

"We're going to look at the way computers have altered our lives," piped up Kevin Green, who's a real swot.

We all groaned. Mrs Weaver thought that we were being rude about Kevin Green and turned to us crossly.

"Well, Francesca, what is your group going to entertain us with?"

My mind went blank. I couldn't think of a thing.

But then Kenny piped up, cool as you like, "We're going to look at medical developments since 1900."

"What?" shrieked Fliss. Blood and gore are just not her thing *at all*.

"It'll be cool, Fliss, trust me!" Kenny grinned.

"Excellent!" smiled Mrs Weaver, clapping her hands. "Books out everyone, it's time to do some maths!"

Kenny nudged me. "Watch this!" she hissed.

Everyone bent down into their bags… and a few seconds later, there was this *terrifying* scream! Emma Hughes ran for the door with awful slime dripping from her hands. Her friend wasn't far behind.

We immediately turned to Kenny.

"Wicked, isn't it? I made up some of our sleepover slime last night," she whispered, grinning madly. "And it was great because it felt just like *snot*. But the best bit is, I added some of Merlin's droppings as well!"

Fliss shuddered. She hates even the *thought* of Kenny's pet rat.

"That's gross!"

"And you poured it into the M&Ms' bags?" squeaked Lyndz. "Fab!"

Mrs Weaver had gone to investigate. When she came back into the classroom, she was mega mad. And so were the M&Ms, who were following behind her.

"I hope that no one in here is responsible for that ridiculous prank," Mrs Weaver barked.

We all looked suitably shocked.

"Because I warn you, I'm going to come down like a ton of bricks if I find anybody engaged in such childish behaviour."

I swear that she looked right at Kenny as she said that. But Kenny just nodded in a really serious way, like she was agreeing with everything Mrs Weaver said. She's got a nerve, that girl!

When we were finally getting on with our work, Rosie whispered:

"We haven't had a slime-fest like that at our

34

sleepovers for ages. We ought to do it at our next one!"

And then I remembered. We hadn't actually planned our next sleepover. And it was going to be the BIG ONE – our New Year's Eve sleepover! I couldn't believe that those stupid M&Ms had made us forget about it! I felt all excited at the thought. But of course, I didn't know then just *how* exciting it was going to turn out to be!

3

The others went into mega-planning mode when I reminded them about the New Year sleepover.

"I can't believe we actually *forgot* about it!" squealed Lyndz. "We've never forgotten about a sleepover before."

Kenny narrowed her eyes and looked menacingly across the playground. "Those M&Ms have a lot to answer for!"

"Chill out, for goodness' sake!" said Rosie, leaping on Kenny's back. "Our sleepover's more important than them. Where are we going to have it? And what are we going to do? We've got to make it really special. Hey, Kenny! *Stop*! Put me down, NOW!"

Kenny had gone racing across the grass outside our classroom with Rosie clinging furiously to her back. The rest of us creased up – they looked hilarious. Only Rosie didn't seem to think so when Kenny finally came back and dumped her on the ground next to us.

"You really are a nutcase!" she fumed. "You could have killed me!"

Rosie can still be a bit too serious sometimes, so there was nothing for it but to tickle her until she begged for mercy.

"But what are we going to do for the sleepover?" asked Fliss at last. "Can't we do something a bit, I don't know – grown-up? I mean, it is kind of special seeing in a new year."

We all agreed that we should do something different, but I knew that we wouldn't be able to agree on anything more than that.

37

"Look, let's ask our parents if we can have a sleepover on New Year's Eve first," I suggested. "Then once we know where we're going, we can decide what we're going to do."

Even as I was saying that, I knew that we wouldn't be having it at my place. I didn't think Mum would mind. But Dad's something else. I mean, ever since he knew that Mum was pregnant, he's been clucking round like a mother hen. He used to be all cool and laid back, then suddenly he went into fusspot overdrive. To hear him talk, you'd think my friends and I were a pack of wild animals out to destroy our house, and scare Mum into the bargain. And he's just got worse and worse. Whenever he starts fussing, Mum just raises her eyes behind his back, and we have a good giggle about it together when he's gone.

Still, I thought I should mention our plan. So that night when I was washing the dishes, I said:

"I don't suppose I could have a sleepover here on New Year's Eve, could I?"

"On New Year's Eve?" Dad plopped a few cups into the soapy water. "I don't think so. I'm not sure my nerves could stand seeing in the new year with all your crazy friends."

But he was smiling as he said it. "Sorry champ!" He ruffled my hair. "Maybe next year. We'll see."

"Yes, sorry Frankie," Mum smiled at me sympathetically. "But I think your dad's probably right."

I wasn't really disappointed, because that's exactly what I'd expected him to say. I just hoped that my friends were having better luck.

When the phone rang a bit later, I knew it'd be for me.

"I'll get it!" I yelled.

"Hi Frankie, it's me, Lyndz." She sounded fed up.

"Don't tell me," I said. "You can't have the sleepover at your place."

"How did you know?"

"It didn't exactly take Sherlock Holmes to suss that one out," I sighed. "You sound really cheesed off. What's up? Why won't they let you have one?"

"Apparently Mum's promised Stuart and Tom that they can have a few of their mates round. I said that was cool because we'd just join in. But Stuart and Tom both said 'No way' and Mum and Dad seemed to agree. Their friends are all stupid morons anyway. I wouldn't want to have a party with them."

Still, poor Lyndz sounded really upset.

"I've had no joy either, because of Mum," I told her. "But don't worry, I'm sure one of the others is having better luck than we are."

"I hope so. See you tomorrow."

I decided to give Kenny a ring to see how she was getting on. Bad move! She was in the middle of a huge row with Molly and her older sister Emma about using the phone. And every time she started to speak to me, the other two started yelling at her.

"I'll ring you back, Frankie," she shouted. Then – silence. The line had gone dead.

"I hope they haven't murdered her," I said, shivering really dramatically when I told Mum and Dad what had happened.

"Her father's probably pulled the phone out of the socket, more like!" Dad laughed. "You do realise that in a few years *we'll* have two people to fight with for the phone?"

He smiled at Mum and patted her stomach and they went all soppy-eyed. They've been doing that a lot lately. I thought I might heave, so I went to my room.

To be honest with you, I didn't give the sleepover much thought that night. I was sure that someone had sorted something out. I kind of hoped that it wasn't Fliss though. She'd make us play stupid games and her mum would make us eat silly little sandwiches. And we wouldn't be able to let our hair down in case we made a mess of her clean and tidy house. I know that sounds awful, but girls just want to have fun sometimes. You know what I mean?

Anyway, as it turned out I needn't have bothered about Fliss, because the next morning she told us that her mum was organising her own party.

"And I don't think she can cope with one of our sleepovers as well," Fliss explained.

41

Lyndz and I rolled our eyes at each other. I don't think Fliss's mum copes with our sleepovers at the best of times.

"Actually," muttered Fliss in her quietest voice, "I thought I might like to stay at home and join in with Mum's party myself. You wouldn't mind, would you? I mean, not having a sleepover on New Year's Eve after all?"

Rosie had joined Lyndz and me by that time, and we all stared at Fliss open-mouthed.

"Of course we'd mind!" I screeched. "You were as excited as any of us about it! And now that something better has come along, you expect us to drop the idea altogether. Well maybe the rest of us will have our sleepover without you!"

I didn't really mean it, but Fliss winds me up sometimes. She always expects us to alter our plans just to suit her. But it looked like our plans were altering anyway. Rosie hadn't had any joy in persuading her mum to let us have the sleepover at her place either.

"She says she'll see," Rosie told us glumly. "And

that usually means she'll pretend to think about it for a fortnight and then tell me the answer's 'no' anyway."

I tried to sound positive. "Let's hope McKenzie comes up with the goods. She usually does."

Typical Kenny. The one morning we were all desperate for her to be early (apart from Fliss, who'd gone off by herself to sulk) was the one morning she was very late. She was so late that Mrs Weaver was about to mark her absent in the register. And Kenny didn't look happy. She didn't look happy at all. In fact, if I didn't know her better, I'd swear that she'd been crying.

We knew by the way that she slammed all her pens on the desk that she was in a bad mood. We were supposed to be finding out about medical developments in the twentieth century for our bit in the play. But Kenny just made loads of doodles in her notebook. And they were all doodles of really gory things, like blood spurting out of hearts and severed legs and stuff. *Awful*!

When break came, I couldn't bear it any longer. As soon as we got outside I tackled her.

"What on earth's the matter with you? Don't tell me – your dad's forbidden you from using the phone ever again?"

"Worse than that. Although he was so angry with us all last night that he did pull the phone out of its socket," Kenny admitted.

I just laughed. "Dad said that's what would have happened."

"Why the long face then?" asked Lyndz.

"I'm not going to be here on New Year's Eve," Kenny blurted out. "We're going up to Scotland to spend it with my grandparents."

What? I just never thought that one of us wouldn't actually be around.

"Well that's it, then. We can't have a New Year sleepover now, can we?" I couldn't bear to see Kenny so miserable.

"Hang on a minute!" It was Fliss. "When I said

that I couldn't come, you said you'd have the sleepover without me. When *she*," she pointed at Kenny, "says she can't come, you say that you can't have a sleepover. That's not fair! You like her better than me, don't you?"

Typical Fliss, only bothered about herself.

"Don't be silly, Fliss. It's different because Kenny really wanted to come and she can't. You told us that you'd rather go to your mum's party," I pointed out. "Besides, we probably wouldn't have had a sleepover without you either."

Fliss smiled weakly.

"I was really looking forward to that sleepover," Kenny mumbled. "I'm sorry that I've let you down."

"Don't be daft. We'll just have to arrange something special for when we're all around." I tried to sound bright, but I was really disappointed too. I'd been convinced that our New Year sleepover was going to be the best yet.

"Still, there is a plus side to all this." Kenny started to grin. "We've got more time to plan

45

our revenge on the M&Ms. I've had a few ideas already…"

We went into a huddle and Kenny outlined her plans to us. And when I say that they were wicked, I mean that in *every* sense of the word. Fliss looked quite pale when she'd heard them.

"I'm not sure about this," she kept whimpering. "I think we might be taking things too far this time. What if we get into trouble?"

Fliss hates the thought of anyone telling her off.

"Look, it's almost the end of term. By the time we put this into practice, there'll only be a couple of days to go. What can anyone do to us then?" reasoned Kenny. "Besides Fliss, they *did* steal your idea for the play. Don't you think that deserves a little revenge?"

Fliss thought for a bit.

"Well I guess so," she admitted slowly. "But I don't want to do any of the risky stuff, OK? And I certainly don't want to get messy."

So I guess you want to know what we did to

the M&Ms then? It was mega, MEGA, *MEGA* brilliant. But Fliss was right to be worried. It did get a bit out of hand.

4

Now as you know, the M&Ms are the yukkiest things on the planet at the best of times. Well, multiply that by a billion and you'll guess how awful they were as we prepared for our end-of-term play. They got up our noses *big* time. They swanked about in their costumes, telling everyone how wonderful they were. And what made it worse was that the clothes they were going to wear were really fab. They had spangly dresses with fringes on them, and dresses with sticky-out skirts.

"This is a proper dress from the 1950s." Emily Berryman twirled round in front of the class. "It belongs to my Auntie Sally. She said she'd lend it to me if I promised to look after it."

Rosie made a being-sick face and Danny McCloud shouted out, "We can see your knickers when you do that!"

The rest of the class collapsed into giggles and Emma Hughes told him to "grow up".

Fliss was getting more and more furious.

"It should have been us in all those great clothes!" she spat. "No one's going to remember our little bit of the play, are they? I mean, 'medical developments since 1900' isn't the most exciting topic in the world, is it?"

Kenny just sighed.

The truth is that none of us were very thrilled when Kenny had suggested our topic for the play. I mean, she wants to be a doctor, so stuff about medical history is fascinating to her. But to the rest of us it was one big YAWWWN. We went round to Kenny's house one night though, and her father told us some really interesting stuff. And he's a doctor, so he knew what he was talking about.

"When you've got a really bad virus, doctors prescribe tablets called antibiotics that fight infection," he told us. "Do you know how their discovery came about?"

Of course, none of us had a clue.

"Well, a man called Alexander Fleming discovered that a particular mould could kill certain nasty germs…"

"A mole? The animal?" asked Rosie.

"No!" he laughed. "A mould, a fungus."

"YUK!" Fliss leapt about ten feet in the air. "Antibiotics aren't made from mould, are they?"

"No, Fliss, things have advanced a bit since then!" he grinned. "But back then, that mould led to the discovery of penicillin, which was really the first type of antibiotic. Now antibiotics save millions of lives."

Fliss was still looking a bit green.

"There are lots of other developments that

aren't to do with illnesses," Dr McKenzie went on. Fliss brightened up a bit.

"I bet your mum's had a lot of scans recently, hasn't she Frankie?" Kenny's dad smiled at me.

I nodded. Since Mum's been pregnant, she's always going to hospital and being hooked up to some machine or other.

"Things like ultrasound machines enable doctors to check out what's going on in the body without doing it any harm," said Dr McKenzie. "It means that we can monitor Frankie's mum's baby and make sure everything's normal. That kind of thing would have been unheard of a hundred years ago. And now we're much better equipped to look after babies if they're born early too. Surely that's a good thing?"

Suddenly, medical developments seemed quite a cool thing to talk about. The others seemed to think so too. Apart from Fliss, who still seemed a bit grossed out about the mould thing.

Anyway, after that we had lots of ideas for our play. The problem was that we were only going to be on stage for five minutes. Ryan Scott and his group were going to be on just before us, with the M&Ms straight after.

"Great!" chortled Kenny when she found out. "It should be easy to put my plan into practice!"

The rest of us looked at each other. The M&Ms certainly deserved what was coming to them, but the end-of-term play was a bit of a risky place to dish it out...

For the next week or so we worked really hard on our performance. We painted loads of boxes so that part of our scenery would look like an old-fashioned laboratory and part of it would look like a high-tech hospital.

Every time the M&Ms saw us rehearsing, they started yawning.

"I bet you'll send everyone to sleep with your bit," they screeched. "But never mind – we'll wake them up with our fashion presentation. Thanks for the idea, Fliss!"

Poor Fliss, I thought she was going to strangle Emma Hughes with her plaits.

"It won't be your stupid fashion show that wakes them up!" muttered Kenny under her breath. The rest of us smirked.

Of course, no one else knew what we had planned, and Mrs Weaver seemed really pleased with our part of the play. Fliss was our narrator, dressed in a white coat to look like a doctor, and Lyndz was going to be Alexander Fleming. We'd saved all this yukky mould from old cheese and fruit and stuff, because Kenny said she wanted it to look realistic. But it was so *gross* that we made Kenny look after it.

Rosie was playing the part of a patient with a nasty virus. First she was going to die a horrible death to show what it would have been like before antibiotics were invented. Then she was going to pretend to be cured by the new drugs. She liked the dying bit best. It seemed to take longer every time we rehearsed it. If we didn't watch out, our entire five

53

minutes would be taken over by her death scene!

For my bit, I was going to be a pregnant woman having an ultrasound scan. Kenny had this great idea of taping a big pink balloon to my tummy so that it looked just like Mum's enormous stomach. Then she was going to be the doctor and smear jelly stuff on to it and pretend to do the scan, just like they do in hospital. It was well cool!

On the evening of the performance, I was really nervous. All our parents were coming to watch, and that suddenly made it all serious. Fliss and Rosie were already at school by the time I arrived, both jiggling about and looking sicky green.

"Come on, you guys!" I tried to jolly them up. "We're only on stage for five minutes and we know what we're doing, don't we?"

They nodded weakly, and I started to blow up the balloon that was going to be my tummy. I'd just got it nice and big and was trying to tie the knot when Lyndz came flying into me. THUD! I ended up on the floor and the balloon went shooting about in the air, making a really rude noise.

"You're disgusting, Felicity Sidebotham!" Emma Hughes sniffed as she walked past.

The thing was – *she wasn't joking*. She hadn't seen the balloon, and she really thought that Fliss had made that noise!!! I was still on the floor, but I was laughing so much I couldn't get up. The more Rosie and Lyndz tried to pull me up, the more we creased up. And what made it worse was that Fliss was just standing there like a goldfish, opening and closing her mouth!

When I eventually got up, my sides ached.

"Can you believe that?" I spluttered. "I'd better go and find my balloon."

"Hurry up!" Lyndz called out after me. "I've got something to tell you!"

I hadn't really seen where the balloon had ended up and no one else had seen it either, so I had to return empty-handed. Fortunately I'd brought a spare one.

55

"What's your news then, Lyndz?" I asked when I got back to the others. I found the other balloon and started to blow it up.

"It's great!" Lyndz was hopping from foot to foot. "But shouldn't we wait until Kenny gets here before I tell you?"

We all looked at each other, then said together, "Nah!", which made us all laugh.

"Well…"

Lyndz was just about to tell us what this great news was when someone thumped me in the back and started shaking a tube of red liquid in front of my face. I nearly swallowed the balloon, which wasn't very funny.

"Don't do that, Kenny!" I yelled, and had to start blowing the balloon up again.

"Look, this is for the operation!" Kenny ignored me and shook the liquid again. "Cool, isn't it?"

"What operation?" I gasped.

"Operation 'Destroy the M&Ms'!" Kenny announced proudly.

"What are you going to do?" shrieked

56

Fliss. "You're not really going to operate on them, are you?"

"Grow up, Fliss!" shrieked Kenny. "It's only for effect!"

"B... but we can't really do anything to them," Fliss stammered. "Not in front of all these people—"

"Don't be such a wet blanket!" Kenny hissed.

Fliss looked as though she was about to cry.

I had finally blown up my balloon and was knotting its neck. "What was your news?" I asked Lyndz quickly, trying to change the subject.

"Crikey, I almost forgot!" Lyndz shrieked. "A sleepover! Mum says we can have one at my place between Christmas and New Year. Then you'll all be able to come! She said, what about Tuesday 28th? We can pretend it's New Year's Eve if we want and do something special. Well, what do you think?"

We all hugged her.

"That'll be great, Lyndz!"

"Yeah, cool!"

57

"Hey, mind my balloon!"

"Places everyone!" Mrs Weaver clapped her hands and started getting everyone organised.

"Don't forget about the M&Ms," Kenny whispered as we made our way to the side of the stage. "Remember the plan!"

Well, if Kenny had a plan, we didn't stick to it. But who cares as long as we made fools of the M&Ms? And we certainly did that. To the max!

5

The first part of our class's performance passed in a bit of a blur. We were so busy trying to calm ourselves down that we didn't watch much of it. Kenny kept disappearing too, and we had no idea what she was up to. I had my own problems with my balloon – somehow it just wouldn't stay taped to my stomach, and it almost floated away twice. The M&Ms of course thought that was hysterical.

"Dolls! Balloons! You're a bigger baby than we thought!" Emma Hughes sneered nastily. She was done up like a dog's dinner in a spangly dress with fringes round the bottom and a feather in her hair. She was practising a stupid dance – 'The Charleston' or something. She said they did it in the 1920s. It looked pretty silly to me, all knocking knees and kicking your legs up. I'd much rather bop along to the Sugababes.

Emily Berryman was still wandering around in her jeans and T-shirt.

"I'm going to wear my Auntie Sally's dress," she growled in her gruff voice. "But I'm not putting it on until the last minute, because I don't want to spoil it. Amanda's keeping an eye on it for me."

"Are you talking about Amanda Porter?" Kenny suddenly reappeared. "I think you'd better go and help her out – she seems to be stuck in her mini-skirt."

The M&Ms twittered off behind the stage.

"Amanda Porter in a mini-skirt! Ugh, gross!" winced Fliss. It wasn't really a pleasant thought.

"I bet they've made her wear a mini-skirt so

that everyone will think how great *they* look," suggested Rosie.

"Amanda's not really stuck, is she?" asked Lyndz suspiciously.

"Yeah!" laughed Kenny. "I accidentally got the zip stuck when I was helping her into her skirt. How else could I tear her away from Berryman's precious dress?"

"What have you done?" I squeaked.

But before she could answer, Mrs Weaver appeared.

"The play's going very well!" She seemed very pleased. "Right, Francesca, can your group please get your scenery together? You're on next."

"I feel sick!" Fliss wailed.

"Don't be such a wimp!" Kenny reprimanded her. "It'll be cool, you'll see!"

Fliss looked as white as a sheet, but I was kind of red and flustered. My balloon was causing me real problems.

We grabbed the boxes we'd painted for our scenery and prepared to go on stage. And getting

61

on stage is where the nightmare *really* began.

We heard the applause for Ryan Scott's group, then a familiar sniggering from the side of the stage, then— TOTAL BLACKNESS. Someone had turned the lights off completely, and we couldn't see anything at all. We were all crashing into each other and treading on each other's toes.

"Ouch, mind my foot!" squealed Fliss's voice.

"Sorry," mumbled Danny McCloud.

There was a crunching sound, then…

"Watch it, you clown!" That was definitely Kenny.

And all the time we were getting totally tangled up in our scenery. When the lights finally went back on – thanks to Mrs Weaver – the stage looked like a battlefield. Ryan Scott was lying dazed on the ground, and Fliss was slumped on top of one of our crushed boxes. People were limping, Rosie was clutching a gash in her shin and Kenny was looking furiously at the M&Ms, who'd collapsed in giggles at the side of the stage. Lyndz had unfortunately started to hiccup, but there was no time to do anything about that.

Red in the face, Mrs Weaver stormed on to the stage and started organising everyone. But I think she was so angry that she didn't really notice what she was doing. So instead of having our own scenery of the hospital, we were surrounded by the televisions and video recorders that the previous group had used for their performance.

As soon as Fliss saw what had happened she started to panic. She turned to Mrs Weaver, but Mrs W just snapped:

"Come on Felicity, I think we've wasted enough time already!"

So Fliss stammered, "Th… there… erm, there have been a great many advances in medicine since 1900…" and at that point Lyndz appeared.

To start with, she was OK and pretended to ignore the fact that she looked like she was standing in a television shop rather than in a laboratory. But when it got to the point where she had to make her discovery about penicillin, she realised that she hadn't got the dish of mould. She looked frantically round at the rest of us.

"Fliss, Fliss..." Kenny hissed. She'd been looking after the mould, hadn't she, and was trying to pass the dish to Fliss. Well, Fliss nearly had a fit when she saw it, and screamed. The yukky green stuff fell out of Kenny's hands and right down Fliss's clean white coat and on to the floor. Fliss started flapping about, trying to wipe the mess off her coat, and the more she flapped, the more the mould got trampled into the stage.

She just looked so funny that the rest of us creased up. Lyndz was giggling and hiccuping at the same time and making this terrible noise, and that just made us worse. Fliss looked really mad at us. She hates being laughed at at the best of times, but in front of all those people too – it was like her *worst* nightmare. Especially as most of the audience were starting to splutter as well. I thought that she might run away, but she didn't. She carried on with her narration.

"Before the invention of antibiotics," she went on bravely, "viruses, which are treatable today, could lead to death."

64

That was Rosie's cue to do her dramatic dying act. She held her head, she gripped her throat, she started to sink to her knees and… *WHOOSH*! She skidded on the patch of mould and fell right off the stage.

I was waiting at the side to come on and do my bit, but as soon as I saw what had happened, I rushed over to Rosie. We all did. The poor thing was all crumpled up on the floor. Fortunately Dr McKenzie had come to watch the play, and he came running over to make sure that she was all right. As he was checking that she hadn't broken anything, Kenny hissed to me:

"The M&Ms are responsible for this! I'm going to fix them *once and for all*…"

"Wait, Kenny!" I yelled, but I forgot that I still had a balloon strapped to my tummy. As I spun round, I fell over – and there was the loudest BANG you've ever heard as the balloon exploded. Everyone went silent. And that's when we heard all the commotion at the back of the stage.

All the boxes, which had been our scenery,

cascaded on to the ground. All apart from two. Kenny and Emma were bashing each other about the head with those. It seemed like everyone else saw what was happening as well, because suddenly they were surrounded by the rest of our class.

"Go, Kenny!" shouted Ryan Scott.

"Hit her, Emma!" squealed Emily.

But Emma suddenly couldn't hit anything, because her feather head-dress had fallen right over her eyes and she couldn't see. She raised the box over her head and stumbled into Kenny. Kenny was caught off balance and fell over – right on top of Emily.

"*Just what is going on here*?" demanded Mrs Weaver, wading through the crowd.

"Kenny's, hic, for it now!" muttered Lyndz, who was standing next to me.

Mrs Weaver's face was like thunder. I'd never seen her so mad.

"I am horrified! I have never…" she began – then Emily Berryman let out this ear-splitting scream.

"I'm bleeding!" she shrieked. "Look!"

Blood was dripping down her arms and falling in a pool on the floor. We looked at Kenny. She had a huge bloodstain spreading over her white coat.

"Kenny, are you all right?" I rushed over to her.

"Oh, that!" She couldn't stop laughing. "It's only red paint. We were going to use it in our play, Mrs Weaver, honestly. The tube must have got broken."

Mrs Weaver looked at her suspiciously.

"I don't remember there being any blood in your performance, Laura," she sniffed. "Emily, do try to calm down, dear. Laura says it's only paint. It will wash off."

But Emily Berryman was wailing harder than ever.

"But look at this!" she cried. "My Auntie Sally's dress is *ruined*!"

We all turned to look. As well as splodges of red paint down the front of the dress, sticky brown blobs were encrusted round the neck and the sleeves.

67

"More of Merlin's droppings!" squealed Rosie, who had hobbled over to join us. "Kenny's done a real job on her this time!"

We thought that Mrs Weaver was going to rip us to shreds, but I guess she thought that wouldn't look too great in front of our parents. Instead she left it for Mrs Poole, the head, to give one of her "I'm-shocked-and disappointed-by-your-behaviour" speeches and to send us all home. And that, of course, is when our parents ripped into us.

"I don't know what to say, Francesca, I really don't." Mum shook her head.

"But it wasn't my fault!" I told her indignantly. "It wasn't me bashing people over the head with cardboard boxes, was it?"

"You're not telling us that you knew nothing about all that business, surely?" said Dad sternly.

But I *honestly* didn't know that was going to happen. All Kenny had planned was tripping up the M&Ms when they were going on stage and bringing the curtain down on them mid-performance, which did all seem pretty tame after that night's display.

"I think you and your sleepover pals are getting a bit out of hand," Dad continued. "Lyndz's mum told us tonight about the sleepover you were going to have to celebrate New Year. Well, that's a definite no-no now."

"But…" I started to protest desperately.

"No buts, Frankie. There'll be no more sleepovers until we can all be sure that you know how to behave."

I couldn't believe my ears. Not only had the M&Ms ruined the play, they'd also ruined my Christmas, my New Year – and my *life*!

6

Well, after Kenny's antics we were all in deepest darkest doom. The way our parents went on at us, you'd think we'd just committed the worst crime in the world. I mean, come on! Nobody died, did they? It's just that things got a bit out of hand. I sometimes think parents were never young themselves, the way they get cross about the slightest thing.

And they weren't the only ones. Boy, was Mrs Weaver furious when we got into school the next day. You could virtually see the steam coming out of her ears. But at least we weren't the only ones she was mad at. Even Emma Hughes couldn't do anything right, which makes a huge change. She's usually Mrs Weaver's very favourite pet – but not on that day.

"Emma Hughes!" she bawled her out. "When I say sit down and be quiet, I mean *everyone* – and that includes you!"

Normally the rest of us would have spluttered with laughter, but we were too terrified. When Mrs Weaver is mad she turns into this fire-breathing monster – and you wouldn't want to cross her, believe me.

"Thank goodness we've only got one more day at school!" muttered Fliss as we were leaving. "I don't think I could take much more of that."

"But that means only one more day of seeing each other," grumbled Rosie. "The way my mum's talking, we're never going to see each other out of school again."

"I was really looking forward to our sleepover

too," admitted Lyndz, in deep gloom.

"Just think, we might have had our last sleepover, ever!" whimpered Fliss.

"Rubbish!" Kenny exploded. "I'm sure I can come up with a plan so that we can still have one!"

The rest of us looked at her in amazement.

"Stop right there!" I turned to her. "It's your plans that got us into this mess to start with, remember. All we can do is be extra good over Christmas, and see if we can talk our parents round."

Kenny tutted and sighed and the others all nodded. But to be honest with you, I didn't hold out much hope. We were well and truly in the doghouse this time.

The next day was really sad, because we figured we wouldn't be seeing each other again until the next term.

"Just think, it'll be *next year* before we see each other again!" marvelled Fliss.

"Yeah, ages away!" Lyndz moaned.

We exchanged our presents and gave each other a hug. Our parents had all come to meet us, because you know what it's like at the end of term – you always seem to have so much stuff to take home. They were all huddled together when we got out of school, which wasn't a good sign. But they seemed happy enough when we joined them. I mean they didn't give us any of those "I-can't-believe-you've-let-me-down-like-this" looks, which was a major improvement from the last few days.

It felt really weird knowing I wouldn't be seeing the others all over Christmas. I know it sounds a bit soppy, but I felt kind of lost without them. Still, there was lots of work to be done around the house. As well as all the usual Christmas stuff, Mum had grand plans for finally sorting out the nursery. Dad had decorated it and everything, but it still wasn't ready for the baby.

"There's still a few weeks to go before it's due," Mum grinned, "but I guess they'll fly by. So we should get it sorted out now."

I bet most people don't spend their Christmas Eve moving boxes around, but that's exactly what we did with ours.

"You won't overdo it, will you, Mum?" I asked anxiously. She was kneeling on the floor, putting away books and files.

"You sound just like your father!" she laughed. "I'm fine. The only problem might be getting me upright again!"

Dad brought my old cot down from the attic, and bags and bags of my baby clothes.

"I can't believe you kept all these!" I squealed as I took out the tiniest, cutest little baby-gros. "Look at these weeny bootees!"

"I can't believe we kept them either," admitted Mum, turning them over in her hands. "They're going to need a good wash."

The doorbell chimed and Dad went to answer it.

"This baby is hardly going to be in the height of fashion, is it? Wearing all these old clothes!" Mum was giggling.

"Speaking of fashion," Dad came back in. "I've

got just the person here to advise you."

"Fliss!" I yelled getting up to hug her. "It's so nice to see you!"

Fliss went pink.

"Ooh, aren't these beautiful?" She bent down to look at the clothes. "They're so tiny and soft. Your baby's going to look so cute!"

"There you are!" laughed Dad. "If Fliss has given them her seal of approval, those clothes are fashionable enough for any baby! But you didn't come to talk about baby fashion, did you Fliss?"

"No!" Fliss blushed. "Mum sent this invitation for you."

She handed over a pretty invitation with embossed silver lettering.

"It's for a special party on New Year's Eve, and you've just got to come, she's got something exciting to tell everybody. Oops, I wasn't supposed to say anything, but you will come, won't you?"

It felt like we'd just been hit by a whirlwind.

"Thank you, Felicity, that's very kind," Mum

75

smiled up at her from the floor. "Tell your mum we'd love to come."

Fliss and I danced around.

"The others are all coming too!" she squealed. "Except Kenny of course, she won't be here."

That put kind of a damper on things. But still, at least I had a party to look forward to.

When Fliss had gone, we tidied everything up in the nursery and went downstairs. Mum turned on the radio and we listened to some carols, joining in when we could remember the words. We had Dad's famous pizza as a treat. And it was kind of cool, sitting there with just the glow from the tree lights brightening the darkness.

"Right champ, time for bed, I think." It was quite late when Dad turned on the main light. "Now you do know that if you make any noise, Father Christmas won't come, don't you?"

"Dad!" I rolled my eyes at him.

"Just make sure you hang up that stocking and go to sleep, OK?"

I gave Mum and Dad a kiss and ran upstairs.

I love Christmas and I couldn't wait to wake up in the morning and open all my presents!

Did I just say I love Christmas? Well pardon me, that was a mistake. What I should have said was I *used* to love Christmas, but not any more. Uh-uh, no way. If I tell you that this Christmas was the biggest nightmare of my life, it wouldn't be any exaggeration at all. You might well look shocked. Well, sit tight while I tell you all about it.

It started off OK. I was awake at the crack of dawn and dived into the stocking at the end of my bed. There was loads of cool stuff in it, like nail varnish and a really great ring I'd wanted for ages. I opened some of the chocolates that were in there too and crept downstairs. It's kind of a tradition in our house that we wait until everyone's there before we open any presents under the tree. So I just had to feel my parcels and try to guess what they were until the oldies finally put in an appearance.

I knew as soon as I saw Mum that something wasn't right. She looked really grey and was kind of wincing when she moved.

"Are you OK?" I asked her anxiously.

"Sure am!" she tried to joke. "I didn't sleep very well, that's all. The baby thought it was party time and started doing the samba. Oooh!"

She doubled over and slumped into a chair.

I was dead worried, but Dad just reckoned she'd overdone it with the clearing up the day before.

"She'll be fine, love," he reassured me, but I could tell that he was concerned too.

That kind of took the edge off my presents really. But I got some great stuff. Fliss had bought me a lovely pair of earrings that looked like butterflies, and Lyndz had bought me a set of megatastic fake tattoos. I got a really cool long scarf from Rosie and a fab new purple pencil case from Kenny because mine was dropping to bits. Mum and Dad gave me loads of clothes and, get this – my own iPod! How cool is that?!

I was really pleased, but all the time I was kind of worried about Mum. Every time I asked how she felt, Mum just said "fine".

It was after we'd eaten Dad's famous Christmas nut roast that it was obvious something was very wrong. Mum kept getting these really bad pains every few minutes and was obviously in agony.

"I think the baby's coming!" she gasped. "We'd better get to the hospital."

I have seriously *never* been so scared in my whole life. I mean, the baby wasn't due for a few weeks, so there must have been something really wrong. What if something awful happened? What if Mum lost the baby? Or what if something happened to Mum? I was so scared I couldn't speak. But I tried not to let Mum see how worried I was. I had to be brave for her sake. So I whizzed round gathering stuff into a bag for her to take into hospital. Then we all piled into the car.

It felt weird. Everyone we passed seemed really happy. There were children out on their new bikes and kids on new rollerblades. And I just wanted to yell, "How dare you look so happy when there's something wrong with my mum?"

I don't think it took very long to get to the hospital, but it seemed like a lifetime. Dad helped Mum out of the car and led her into the Maternity unit.

"She will be all right, won't she Dad?" I squeezed his hand as some nurses led Mum away.

"Of course. She's in the right place now!" Dad smiled and gripped my hand tighter.

As we sat in the waiting room, there seemed to be loads of babies crying, which just reminded me about Mum.

"Do you fancy a cup of tea, love?" Dad asked after we'd been sitting staring at the wall for ages.

I nodded. He went down the corridor to a machine and I waited for him. Suddenly a woman in a white coat came into the room.

"Ah, you must be Frankie Thomas. I'm Dr Wilson," she smiled and held out her hand. I was sure that she was going to tell me something awful, but she just laughed. "Don't look so worried, everything's

80

fine. We've just been running a few tests on your mum and… oh hello, you must be Gwyn?"

Dad had just come through the door with two steaming cups of tea.

"I was just telling Frankie here that Helena's absolutely fine. The baby's doing great too. You can go and see her now if you like."

I started running down the corridor, until I remembered where I was and just made myself walk really fast. I almost threw myself at Mum when I got to her room, I was so pleased to see her.

"Hey, there you are!" she beamed and ruffled my hair. "Sorry I've messed up your Christmas Day, Frankie. I bet you didn't expect to spend it in a hospital, did you?"

I shook my head, and tears started to roll down my face.

"I'm sorry, darling," she said, giving me a big hug.

I wasn't crying because I was feeling sorry for myself. I was crying because I was so relieved.

"I'm just glad you're all right," I sniffed. "And the baby too."

81

"It was probably a touch of indigestion," confirmed Dr Wilson. "These things can happen in the later stages of pregnancy."

We all looked at Dad.

"OK, OK, no more pizzas or nut roasts!" he laughed, holding up his hands. "I know that you both think my cooking stinks, but this was rather a drastic way of telling me, don't you think? Everything we eat from now until the baby's born will definitely be out of a packet, I promise!"

It felt so good to get out of hospital and back home. It was dark by that time and it felt really strange, like I hadn't had a Christmas Day at all. Mum kept saying that she was sorry and that she'd make it up to me, but all I wanted was for her to be all right. What did it matter if I'd missed Christmas for one year?

7

Well, it seems that even if *I* wasn't bothered about missing Christmas Day, Mum was bothered for me. She spent most of Boxing Day on the phone and she wouldn't tell me who she was calling.

"Is that Gran?" I asked as I passed her in the hall. She shook her head and wouldn't even tell me who it was when she'd finished. After that, she sneaked into Dad's office to make all her calls. And if the phone rang she shouted, "That's for me!" and lumbered into the office to get it.

"You're acting really weird, Mum," I told her when she finally sat down. "Are you sure they didn't give you any funny medicine when you were at the hospital?"

"Don't be rude!" she smirked. "All will be revealed soon enough."

I was still kind of worried about her, and to tell you the truth I didn't think all this cloak-and-dagger stuff would be doing her any good at all. But Dad didn't seem too worried about it. In fact, he seemed to be joining in. At one stage I could have sworn I heard Lyndz's father's van outside. Dad disappeared and returned about five minutes later saying it was only someone asking for directions. It was all very strange.

On Monday, the day after Boxing Day, my gran came over from Nottingham, which was great. She brought loads of presents with her and fussed around Mum.

"You know you really should have taken it easier," she scolded her. "Having a baby at your age was never going to be easy. I'm not

84

surprised you had a scare like that."

Mum rolled her eyes, and for a moment she looked like a little schoolgirl who'd just been told off.

"So when are you going to be seeing all those nice friends of yours, Francesca?" Gran turned to me. (She can never quite bring herself to call me Frankie.)

"I don't know," I shrugged. "On New Year's Eve, probably."

I saw Mum and Dad look at each other. I figured they'd decided that Fliss's mum's party might be too exciting for Mum after what had just happened.

"It doesn't matter if you don't want to go," I told them quickly. "I'm not bothered about it, honestly. I don't mind not seeing my friends."

Mum and Dad burst out laughing.

"We'll have to tell her now, won't we!" Mum said at last.

"Tell me what?" I asked anxiously. "You are all right, aren't you Mum? You're not going to have to go into hospital again, are you?"

"Hey, calm down!" grinned Dad. "Since when have you been Miss Frankie Freak-Out? Your mum's fine, aren't you love?"

"Course I am," Mum reassured me. "You heard what the doctor said – I've just got to avoid your dad's cooking for a while!"

"Thanks!" Dad guffawed. "Anyway, we weren't going to tell you yet but…"

"Your sleepover's back on!" Mum blurted out. "I couldn't bear to think of you missing out on all your celebrations, so I rang everyone up yesterday. You'll be having your early New Year sleepover at Lyndz's tomorrow after all."

I didn't know what to say – I was absolutely *stunned*.

"You're the greatest!" I squealed when I'd found my voice. I grabbed hold of Mum and Dad in a big hug, then grabbed hold of Gran too. She looked totally bewildered by everything.

When I'd finally calmed down, Dad went into his office and came back holding an envelope.

"Lyndz's dad dropped this off for you yesterday. It's an invitation, I think."

I quickly opened it, and as I pulled out the invitation, hundreds of tiny glitter snowflakes fell on to the floor.

Lyndz invites you to a
SPECIAL (EARLY)
NEW YEAR'S EVE SLEEPOVER
DRESS TO IMPRESS
AND
BRING EXOTIC AND TEMPTING GOODIES
FOR THE SPECIAL MIDNIGHT FEAST!

Please arrive at 6pm

How cool was that?! She must have made it specially, as soon as she knew that the sleepover was back on again.

"I'll have to decide what to wear!" I shrieked, dashing up to my room.

The invitation said 'Dress to Impress'. Now what on earth did that mean? I was dying to know what the others were going to be wearing, but I didn't want to ring them. I wanted it all to be a big surprise. Usually we have our sleepovers when we've just been at school together. This time I wouldn't have seen the others for over a week, and I reckon that's some kind of record for us. I couldn't wait to see them again. But first I had the little problem of my outfit to sort out!

It's a good thing that Mum and Dad didn't spring this sleepover on me at the last minute – it took me absolutely *ages* to decide what to wear. My bedroom looked as though a hurricane had hit it by the time I'd got my outfit sorted. Mind you, it was worth it! I put on a skinny-rib black top and black mini-skirt, then draped a

88

couple of big chiffon scarves over the top of them, so they sort of floated away from my body as I moved. I had my best spiky-heel shoes on and masses of necklaces. As I twirled in front of the mirror I was well pleased.

"Yep, Frankie, you're certainly dressed to impress now, girl!" I told my reflection.

There was a knock at the door.

"Talking to yourself is the first sign of madness, you know," Mum laughed. Then she came into my room.

"Frankie! My goodness, what a tip!"

Poor Mum! You ought to have seen her face.

"I'll tidy it up, don't worry. You go and sit down!" I tried to shoo her away.

"I didn't realise getting dolled up was such a messy business!" Mum sighed. "That must have been where I've been going wrong all these years!"

"Well, Mum, you've either got it or you haven't!" I pretended to swank about.

"And you'll have an earful from your dad if you don't clear this room up sharpish!"

89

I changed out of my party outfit and hung it up carefully. Then Mum and I tackled the rest of my room. When we'd finished Mum said:

"I loved your outfit by the way! You looked really grown-up."

I gave her a big hug. "Thanks, Mum."

We had an early tea so that Gran could get home before it got too late. She doesn't really like driving in the dark, you see. But I think Mum and Dad were relieved when she did leave, because she'd been fussing over Mum ever since she arrived. She kept going on about how she was kind of old to be having another baby and how she hoped that Christmas Day hadn't been a warning. Mum was getting wound up, I could tell, and Dad just kept calling Gran "The Prophet of Doom" to make her shut up. But what she said kind of got to me, and I started to worry about Mum all over again.

In fact, I got myself into such a state that I almost didn't go to the sleepover. On Tuesday evening I'd got dressed and packed my stuff and everything – and then I suddenly thought: what would I do if Mum had to go into hospital again and I didn't know anything about it?

"Relax, Frankie!" Mum said when I told her how I felt. "I have no intention of going into hospital yet. And if anything does happen, anything at all, we'll ring you at Lyndz's."

"You promise?"

"Promise!"

"Why is it women are always late?" Dad stomped into the lounge. "I've been waiting for you in the car for five minutes."

"I wasn't sure that I was going to go to the sleepover," I told him.

"And let the others miss out on seeing you in all your finery? You must be mad!" Dad smiled. "Don't worry about your mum, Frankie, I'll look after her. And we won't let you miss anything, honestly!"

I felt better after they'd reassured me, but a tiny part of me still felt that I shouldn't be going out and leaving them. But you know what? I felt better as soon as I got to Lyndz's.

I was the last to arrive, and when I knocked on the door there was this stampede to open it. And *wow*! You should have seen what the others were wearing!

Lyndz had had the pick of her dressing-up clothes and was wearing this brilliant Spanish dress with millions of flounces down the skirt. She had this totally cool comb thing in her hair too. Kenny had really excelled herself by wearing a new Leicester City shirt *and* a Leicester City tracksuit top – no surprises there! Rosie was all done up in some of her sister Tiffany's clubbing gear, which looked really wild. She was wearing this leopard-print mini skirt and a sort of rubber bodice thing. But I think she felt a bit uncomfortable in that because she kept trying to tug it down. But the coolest thing was she'd stuck a blue 'jewel' into her tummy button with some special glue and it sort of sparkled whenever she moved. It was *wicked*.

But Fliss took the biscuit. Her mum had actually bought her – yes, *bought* her – a slinky electric-blue evening dress. Her make-up was immaculate, and she looked as though she'd spent the whole day in a beauty parlour.

"I'm really trying it out for Mum's New Year's Eve party!" she smirked when I told her how great she looked. "It was ever so expensive and I wouldn't normally wear it to one of our sleepovers…"

"Charming!" sniffed Lyndz.

"…but," Fliss carried on, "seeing as this is a special sleepover, I thought I might as well. It's the first time I've ever worn it properly, so you're all honoured!"

"Thanks very much, Fliss!" we all laughed sarcastically. But she thought we were being serious and said, "You're welcome!" which made us all laugh even more. Honestly, what is she like?!

It felt really good being with the others again. And I know that the others felt the same, because for a few minutes we just stood there grinning at each other. But Kenny of

course was soon keen to see some action.
She leapt on to Lyndz's back and yelled at the
top of her voice:

"Let the party begin!"

8

Before we could get on with the fun part of the sleepover, we had to take all our stuff up to Lyndz's room. Now, I don't know if you remember, but Lyndz's house is all higgledy-piggledy. Her dad is always in the middle of doing some major building project or other, so her house is always in a bit of a state. I don't mean that in a nasty way, I just mean that – well, you don't usually find great planks of wood and old doors propped up in the lounge, do you?

And I bet your house has carpet on the floor, doesn't it? There are just dirty old floorboards at Lyndz's, which freaks Fliss out big time!

Lyndz's bedroom is really tiny, and Kenny always jokes that her rat Merlin lives in a bigger *cage*! But Lyndz knows that she's only teasing. Besides, her dad's building her a spanking new room right at the top of the house. She swears that it's going to be ginormous when it's finished. At the moment, when we all pile into her room we're like a row of sardines in a can! She has to take out her bed, just so that we can all fit in. But we don't mind because we always have a really cool time when we're at Lyndz's. And this time was certainly no exception.

"WOW! Look at this!" we gasped as soon as we got into her room. There were banners all over the wall saying HAPPY NEW YEAR! and helium-filled balloons were tied up at each corner. It was wicked!

"We'd already got the banners for Stuart and Tom's party," admitted Lyndz. "I just sort of borrowed them."

"Won't they mind?" asked Fliss anxiously. I think

she's a bit scared of Lyndz's older brothers because they're always teasing her.

"Nah, they'll never know!" Lyndz smiled a little nervously. "They never set foot in my room anyway, so I'll just take them down tomorrow and put them back in the bag."

"Clever you!" Kenny teased, and started tickling her.

Now tickling and Lyndz mean just one thing. Yep, you've guessed it – hiccups! It was really hysterical because the more she hicced, the more the comb thing on her head moved around. It looked like a bird or something pecking at her head. We doubled up, it just looked so funny. Lyndz didn't know what we were laughing about until we pointed to her reflection in the mirror. And that of course just made things worse. She got redder and redder and tears started streaming down her face.

"We ought to do something!" Fliss was looking quite concerned.

Suddenly there was a knock on the door.

"What's going on in there?" It was Stuart.

"Quick! Don't let him come in!" squealed Lyndz. We all bustled out of the door.

"Out of the way, Stu!" Lyndz barged past her brother. "We've got a party to get on with!"

Stuart just shook his head as we all bundled downstairs.

"Your hiccups have gone!" whispered Rosie when we were in the lounge.

"It must have been the thought of Stuart coming into my room and seeing those banners!" Lyndz giggled. "He'd have my guts for garters if he knew I'd borrowed them! Right then, anybody fancy a dance?"

She rushed over to the corner and turned on the CD player. This awful thumping sound blasted out so loud, I swear the walls started shaking.

"Aw man, that's dreadful!" Kenny yelled, covering her ears with her hands.

"Sorry about that," Lyndz grimaced when she'd managed to turn it off. "It's some of Tom's awful techno stuff."

"I'm glad we're not coming to the party here on New Year's Eve if that's what they're going to be listening to," Rosie told her.

"We're going to have great music at our party," Fliss gushed. "Mum went out and bought loads of new CDs. It's going to be perfect!"

I looked across at Kenny. We usually pull faces at each other when Fliss goes off on one of her "I-am-wonderful" speeches, but Kenny was looking really miserable. Lyndz must have noticed too, because she put on a CD and turned it up really loud to drown out Fliss. Then she grabbed Kenny's arm and made her dance.

It was cool bopping around. We could have done without Lyndz's little brother Ben joining us, though. He's a right little tearaway, and thought it would be fun to start pelting us with fruit. A satsuma caught Kenny right on the back of the head.

"This means war!" Kenny muttered through gritted teeth, and grabbed a bunch of grapes from the fruit bowl. "Right, young Benjamin, how d'you fancy this lot crushed over your bonce?"

Soon we were all charging round the room armed with handfuls of fruit. Fliss looked very uneasy.

"Ooh, that reminds me, Mum made me an exotic fruit salad for our midnight feast," she suddenly piped up. "It's in my bag and I really should put it in the fridge. I'll just pop up to get it."

"Typical Fliss!" Kenny shouted across to me. "That girl just doesn't know how to have fun!"

A couple of walnuts came flying across the floor and hit me right in the shin.

"Yow! That really hurt!" I stumbled over to the sofa and rubbed my leg.

"Right, that's it Ben, I'm going to tell Mum!" Lyndz stormed out to the kitchen.

The others crowded round me, and *wallop* – a fig landed on Rosie's lap.

"I'm going to get you!" Kenny yelled, narrowing her eyes as she looked at Ben. She grabbed a really squashy kiwi fruit from the fruit bowl and aimed it towards him. He bobbed down behind an armchair and *splat*! The kiwi fruit hit the wall. As if that wasn't bad enough, Fliss had just reappeared, and the sight of a kiwi fruit hurtling towards her made her stumble. Unfortunately the lid wasn't securely on her container of fruit salad and a little bit of the juice slopped down her dress.

Tom, of course, chose just that moment to put in an appearance.

"Oh, Fliss, you haven't wet yourself, have you?" he smirked. "That's a pity, you were looking pretty good too – for one of Lyndz's friends!"

"That's enough, Tom!" Lyndz's mum came in. "Benjamin Collins! I hear you're causing a nuisance." She grabbed his hand and dragged him out.

"It might be an idea to pick some of that fruit off the floor, girls," she shouted over her shoulder. "We wouldn't want any accidents if you slipped on it!"

I told you that we always have a cool time at Lyndz's! Any other parents would have gone ballistic if they'd found fruit slung all over their lounge. I know that *my* parents would – wouldn't yours?

"We could put some of this in your fruit salad, Fliss," giggled Rosie, scooping up a squashy tangerine. "The dirt might give it a bit of crunch!"

The rest of us cracked up, but Fliss was still upset about her dress.

"The best thing to do is leave it and let it dry naturally," said Lyndz kindly. "I bet if you dance around in it really fast, it'll dry in no time and we won't be able to see the mark at all."

"Do you think so?" asked Fliss.

"Oh yes!" we all nodded confidently.

Well, it was a good excuse for a dance, wasn't it? So when we'd cleaned up all the fruit, we did the routines we knew for the Sugababes and Britney Spears. And then we put on our favourite bopping tunes.

I was pretty exhausted, not to mention hungry, when Lyndz's mum called us through for supper. She'd laid out a table so it looked like a really swanky dinner party. We had our Coke in proper wine glasses and everything.

After we'd eaten, we watched *High School Musical*, and then pretended that we were some of the characters. I don't know what time it was when Lyndz suggested we get ready for bed.

"I thought we were going to see in our 'New Year' like this," complained Fliss, smoothing down her dress. "I wouldn't have worn it otherwise."

I was kind of ready to get into my jim-jams, and I figured the others were too.

"Well, you know Fliss, I think you should save that dress for seeing in the *proper* New Year," I reasoned. "It's so beautiful, and you wouldn't want to risk spoiling it again with our midnight feast, would you? You know what a messy eater Kenny can be!"

Kenny pretended to bop me on the head, but at least Fliss agreed to get ready for bed.

I must admit it felt kind of nice to slob out after we'd been so dressed up. After we'd washed and everything, we wriggled into our sleeping bags, then sat up in them so we could see each other. As I told you, the room is so small that it took a while for us all to get comfortable.

"I know! Why don't we tell each other what we want to happen in the New Year?" suggested Fliss.

"Well, I just want the baby to arrive safely," I told the others. "And for it to be healthy and for Mum to be OK."

"I'm sure everything will be fine," Lyndz reassured me. "What about you, Kenny, what do you want?"

"I want to finish the M&Ms off once and for all!" she yelled.

"Yes!" We all agreed with that.

"But what else do you want, Kenny?" Rosie asked when we'd all calmed down.

"Leicester City to win the FA Cup," she grinned. We all groaned. "And for me to get into a proper football team and for my skills to be spotted and to play for England and…"

"Yes, we get the picture!" we laughed, bashing her with our pillows.

"Well, what I want more than anything is actually

going to happen!" squealed Fliss. Then she added, in that *really* annoying way of hers, "But I can't tell you what it is!"

The rest of us looked at each other.

"That's what you think!" said Kenny menacingly. We all wriggled in our sleeping bags over to Fliss and started to tickle her.

"We have ways of making you talk!" giggled Rosie, tickling Fliss right under her arms.

"Get off!" she squawked. "That's not fair! I'm not telling you. I promised!"

"Promised who? Who did you promise?" demanded Kenny.

"Don't tell me you're going to marry Ryan Scott!" I joked.

By then we were all kind of breathless, so we collapsed back into our sleeping bags. Fliss was looking really chuffed with herself for not giving in to us. But as soon as we mentioned her beloved Ryan's name, she want all pink and peculiar.

"No silly! But oh, I almost forgot... now, where

is it?" Fliss was in a real tizzy of excitement, trying to rummage about in her bag.

"Ah here it is!" She pulled out a Christmas card of two robins nestling together on a branch and started wafting it about in front of our faces. "Well, did anyone else get one of these?"

"Yep, I think we can all say that we got plenty of cards, Fliss," Rosie said, pulling a face.

"No, look who it's from!" Fliss squealed and pointed to the signature at the bottom.

Luv Ryan

"You are joking!" I screeched. "Is this for real or is it a joke?"

I looked at the old prankster Kenny, but she looked as mystified as the rest of us. Fliss just blushed and went all soppy. There was going to be absolutely no dealing with her now.

"What about you, Rosie, what do you want in the New Year?" I asked.

"Well, I used to wish for my parents to get back together again," she admitted. "But now I know that they're both happier with the way things are.

So I guess I'd like the rest of the house to be decorated. You lot don't fancy helping, do you?"

"No way!" laughed Kenny. Talk about hard work!"

"I guess that's what I'd like too," admitted Lyndz. "I want Dad to finish my new room, so that we'll have more space for our sleepovers!"

"That's what we want too!" shouted Kenny. "I'm getting cramp here being squashed in next to you lot!"

We were just going to pile on top of her when we heard something outside Lyndz's door.

"Have you seen the time, girls?" Lyndz's mum called.

"BONG…" Tom and Stuart were pretending to sound like Big Ben.

"It must be midnight!" squealed Rosie.

"BONG…"

"What should we do now?" asked Fliss anxiously.

"BONG…"

"You're supposed to sing some special song, but I don't know the words," I told them.

"BONG…"

"Well, let's all get in a group hug then," suggested Lyndz. "We've got to do *something*."

We all got into a huddle. And when Stuart and Tom had bonged twelve times, we hugged each other extra hard and yelled, "*Happy New Year!*"

Then Lyndz's mum and dad, Stuart and Tom burst through the door. Her mum was carrying a tray with a bottle of lemonade done up like champagne and five posh glasses. They were grinning all over their faces – until Stuart noticed the banners on the walls.

I really thought all hell was going to break loose when Stuart spotted the decorations.

"Are those *my* banners?" he asked suspiciously.

"Well, erm, yes," stuttered Lyndz. "I'm only borrowing them, I didn't think you'd mind—"

"Of course I mind!" he yelled. "Mum made me use my own money to buy them, and you didn't even *ask* to borrow them!"

"Well, I knew you wouldn't lend them to me if I did!" Lyndz was getting a bit upset, I could tell.

"Too right I wouldn't," Stuart snapped back. "I know you and your mad friends. You're bound to ruin them with your stupid games."

Rosie mumbled "Charming" under her breath, but he didn't seem to hear.

"Well, I'm going to take them down right now!"

Before anyone could stop him, Stuart stormed right into the room. He grabbed one end of a banner and tugged it, but I guess he'd forgotten that there were five sleeping bags on the floor. He certainly hadn't bargained on Fliss being inside hers. She'd snuggled back inside at the first sign of trouble. Anyway, Stuart tripped over her and stumbled. The banner was still in his hand as he fell, and with a SNAP the string broke and the letters spelling out HAPPY NEW YEAR! fell to the floor like autumn leaves.

We just stood there and didn't know what to do. Fliss was squealing and trying to get Stuart's foot out of her hair, Lyndz looked as though she was about to burst into tears and Tom was laughing his head off.

"Well, your New Year's certainly started with a bang!" observed Lyndz's mum, putting the tray with the glasses down on Lyndz's table. "Or should that be a bump?"

"So much for *Lyndz*'s silly games spoiling your banners, Stu," said Mr Collins, helping Stuart up from the floor. Stuart was bright red and looked furious with Lyndz.

"You really should have asked him first though, you know Lyndsey." Lyndz's mum sounded serious, but then she added, "You'd better toast in the New Year before anything else happens!"

When Lyndz's parents, Stuart and Tom had left, us we all looked at each other. Then Kenny cracked up.

"That was class! Did you see Stu fall?"

"*Felt* him, more like!" moaned Fliss, although she was grinning. "Your brother is one big lump, Lyndz!"

That seemed to cheer Lyndz up. She poured out our lemonade and we wished each other a "Happy New Year" as we clinked glasses.

When we finally settled down to sleep, Fliss

said, "Your mum was right though. It wasn't a great start to a New Year, was it? Let's hope we have better luck with the real one!"

"Except I won't be there, will I?" mumbled Kenny quietly. "You'll all be starting the New Year together and I'll be in Scotland."

She sounded really miserable.

"But we'll toast you, won't we guys?" I comforted her.

"Sure will!" the others agreed. Kenny seemed kind of thrilled about that, but still a bit sad.

Saying goodbye to each other in the morning was pretty hard because we knew that we'd next see each other at Fliss's party and Kenny wouldn't be there. It didn't seem right, somehow.

Still, I was relieved to get home, just so I could reassure myself that Mum was OK.

"Did you have fun, darling?" she asked.

"Yes, it was coo-ell!" I told her all about the fruit fight and the lemonade at midnight and Stuart getting mad and falling over.

"And you should have seen Fliss's dress!" I gabbled. "Well, you will, won't you? She'll be wearing it at her mum's party."

"Ah yes, the party!" Mum said sarcastically. "Nikki rang last night in a bit of a flap."

"When *isn't* Fliss's mum in a bit of a flap?" I asked.

"Well, she's in a lot of a flap actually," Mum continued. "She was having a major crisis about some napkins, so I said she could borrow some of ours. You wouldn't mind taking them round this afternoon, would you Frankie?"

Now, going round to Fliss's house when her mum's in a tizz is not exactly high on my list of fun things to do. But it didn't really look as though I had much choice. So later that afternoon, armed with a carrier bag full of napkins, I set off.

It was obvious as soon as I got to the door that things were not exactly rosy inside. I could hear a high-pitched squeaking that at first I thought was

Fliss, but then Fliss bundled out of the front door all red in the face.

"Are you OK?" I asked.

"Oh, Frankie, thank goodness!" Fliss grabbed hold of my arm. "Mum's going off on one. You should hear her!"

"I think I just have," I admitted. I could still hear the squeaking, but it was getting louder. It was coming closer. It was Fliss's mum!

"Don't you dare run away from me, Felicity!" she squeaked. Then she saw me. "Ah, Frankie, I don't think I'm going to need those napkins now. I've decided I'm not having a party, it's too much to cope with. Too much food, too many people, too much mess. I wish I'd never told anyone about it. I don't think I can face it, I really don't."

It was amazing. I mean, the woman never stopped to draw breath! And boy, did she look rough! Usually she's dead trendy, but not today. Today she made King look like Naomi Campbell. I knew something must be really wrong because she hadn't even bothered to put any make-up on.

She usually wears enough to supply the cosmetics counter at Boots.

"You can't cancel the party now, Mrs Sidebotham," I told her, alarmed. "Everyone's really looking forward to it."

Fliss's mum's chin began to wobble and she started to sniff. I wasn't sure that I could face seeing her break down in tears. It's bad enough coping with Fliss when she's like that.

"Why don't I make you a cup of tea?" I suggested, as Fliss and I steered her towards the kitchen.

And that was another sign that Fliss's mum wasn't quite right – she actually let me into the house without me taking my shoes off first. And that almost *never* happens. But I wished I hadn't thought about it, because you know how your mind sometimes wanders? Well, mine went on a major expedition! I kept thinking how funny it would be if Mrs Sidebotham made everyone take off their shoes when they came to the party. There'd be a great pile of them by the door and they'd all get muddled up and everyone would end up going home in the wrong pair…

"What's so funny?" demanded Fliss as we got into the kitchen. I hadn't even realised that I was smiling. But fortunately, before I had a chance to explain, Andy and Callum appeared, carrying huge boxes piled high with bags of crisps and things.

"Hiya, Frankie, how are you?" Andy beamed at me and dumped his box on the breakfast bar.

"Fine thanks," I smiled back at him. I really like Andy. He's Fliss's mum's boyfriend, but we tend to think of him as Fliss's stepfather because he's been around forever. Even Fliss calls him her stepfather sometimes. Anyway, he's always really bright and cheerful, and I've no idea how he manages that, living with Fliss and her mum – not to mention Callum!

Mrs Sidebotham was slumped on one of the stools next to the breakfast bar, and as Andy and Callum carried in more and more boxes from the car, she started to whimper again.

"Oh, I can't cope with this, I just can't!" she wailed. "We're going to have to call the party off!"

"Now, now, we've been over this," murmured Andy soothingly, putting an arm around her shoulder. "We're having someone in to prepare the food. We've bought all the drinks, the house is clean, the decorations are still up from Christmas, and we're here to help out, aren't we guys?"

Fliss and Callum nodded solemnly.

"So you see, all you have to do is look beautiful, my love." Andy kissed Fliss's mum on the cheek. "And you can't help doing that, can you? This party is definitely going ahead, because I want to show you off!"

Yuk! I thought I was going to throw up, I really did, but at least Mrs Sidebotham was smiling again.

"And besides, Mum, you've got to have the party because you want everyone to know about…" Fliss bent over and whispered something in her mum's ear. I don't know what it was, but Mrs Sidebotham went all giggly and pink.

After that she went back into traditional 'Fliss's mum' mode. You know, twittering about and fussing over where to put things so they wouldn't get broken. That was definitely my cue to leave.

"I'll see you at the party, then?" I called as I left.

"OK, sweetie, thanks for the napkins!" Mrs Sidebotham called out from the lounge. It was like she'd totally forgotten all about the state she was in when I first got there.

Fliss came to the door with me.

"Thanks for coming, Frankie. I think Mum's excited, that's all!"

"Yeah, course," I nodded. I was just glad that *my* mum didn't go off on one whenever she was excited.

"I wonder what the party's really for?" I asked Mum when I got home. "Fliss's mum's certainly all ga-ga about something, and it's definitely not just New Year's Eve."

"If it's what I think it is, Nikki will want to make it a party to remember!" Mum replied.

Well, let me tell you, none of us will *ever* forget that New Year's Eve party. But I don't think it was exactly what Fliss's mum had in mind!

10

When the day of the party finally came round, I was well up for it. I suppose I was excited because it was the first grown-up party I'd ever been to, and I didn't really know what to expect. I just figured it would be sophisticated and glamorous and—

"Boring!"

That's what Dad said, anyway. He reckons that whenever grown-ups get together, all they talk about is how tiring their jobs are and how much money they spend. Great! I was in for a really fun evening, wasn't I? I didn't take much notice of him actually, because I think he was just trying to put me off. I don't think he and Mum were really looking forward to Fliss's mum's party.

I was kind of hyper as soon as I got up, but I knew that I had a whole day to get through before we went out, so I thought of all the things I could do to calm me down. The first thing on my list was to ring Kenny. I was sure that she said they were going to drive up to her grandparents in Scotland at about ten in the morning of New Year's Eve. But when I rang her at nine, there was no reply.

"They probably set off early," Mum suggested. "It's quite a drive up there."

"They might even have gone up last night," Dad chipped in. "I'm not sure I'd want to drive all that way and be thrown straight into the Hogmanay celebrations. It gets pretty wild up there, I gather."

"Kenny will fit in well then!" I chuckled.

"Ooh, I've just had a vision of Kenny doing

121

the Highland fling!" groaned Dad. "Now that's not a pretty sight at breakfast time!"

"Dad!" I laughed, and punched him on the arm.

I was a bit miffed that Kenny hadn't rung me before she left, though. But then again, she had been kind of upset knowing that we would all be together on New Year's Eve without her. Perhaps she was still a bit cut up about it.

When the phone rang a little later I pounced on it, expecting it to be Kenny. Wrong! It was Fliss's mum and she was in another tizz. In fact, we are talking Panic City!

"Ooh Frankie, is your mum around, only…"

I held the phone out to Mum and mouthed "Fliss's mum!"

Mum rolled her eyes and took the receiver. "Hello, Nikki, are you ready for the party then?"

Stupid question, Mother. Mum was on the phone for *forty minutes*, trying to reassure Fliss's mum that yes, she was sure she had enough food, and no, she didn't think there would be any gatecrashers, and… Well, you get the picture, don't you? Poor Mum looked shattered when she got off the phone.

But if *that* wasn't bad enough, Fliss's mum kept ringing back. When the phone rang for the fifth time, Mum said:

"Will you get that, Frankie? And if she asks for me, tell her I've gone to the doctor's with earache!"

"Mum!" I pretended to look shocked and picked up the receiver.

"Hi, Mrs Sidebotham, I'm afraid Mum's had to pop out," I fibbed. "Yes, I'll tell her you rang. See you tonight then, bye."

"My father always told me it was wrong to lie," I said in a sickly-sweet voice when I'd put the phone down.

"Well, Frankie, there are nasty big lies and there are little white ones that might just save someone's sanity…"

"…and that was one of those, right?" I asked seriously.

"You bet your life it was. I'm going to lie down,

I feel exhausted." Mum pretended to clutch her head and swept dramatically out of the room.

I don't know how I got through the rest of the day without going crazy. I tried on my outfit about a million times (I'd decided to wear what I'd worn to our sleepover), and experimented with loads of different make-up. I picked out one of the fake tattoos Lyndz had bought me, then decided to have a bath before I put it on. And all the time excitement was kind of bubbling inside me.

When it finally got to early evening and Dad was fixing us all something to eat, I could barely contain myself.

"Do you think there'll be dancing? I can't imagine Fliss's mum dancing, can you? Ooh, thanks Dad, veggie bangers, my favourite! Do you think there'll be lots to eat there tonight? I mean, am I going to be too full up if I eat these now?" I babbled on, barely pausing for breath. "Oh, Mrs Sidebotham won't have those silly little sandwiches, will she? What's up, Mum, aren't you eating anything? Are you saving yourself for the food later?"

"No, I think I'll just have a piece of bread or something," Mum said quietly. "I've just got a touch of indigestion again. Nothing to worry about."

"Nikki's worn you down with all her fussing hasn't she?" Dad turned to Mum and started rubbing her back. "Never mind – after tonight it'll all be over. We probably won't see Nikki for a month, she'll be in such a state of shock after all those people have trampled through her house!"

"Aw, don't say that, Dad! I'm looking forward to this party, even if no one else is," I told them defiantly. "Do you think you can teach me the words for that song you sing at midnight, 'Old Land Signs' or whatever it's called? I don't want to be the only one who doesn't know the words."

Mum and Dad looked at each other.

"The song's called 'Auld Lang Syne'," Dad explained. "But I don't think you'll be needing the words for that. We're only popping along to the party for a couple of hours, you know. We'll be home well before midnight."

"What?!" I yelled. "What's the point of going

to a New Year's Eve party if you don't stay till midnight? This is, like, a new year!"

I was really, *really* gutted. I mean, I'd been building up to this party for a week, and they had to choose now, like an hour before we went, to drop the bombshell that we were only "popping along", like it was a tea party or something!

"All the others will be staying. It's not fair!" I knew that I was whining and that I must sound like Fliss. But I didn't care.

"Well, if you're going to behave like a spoilt child, we needn't go at all." Dad was looking at me sternly over the rim of his glasses. "We thought you were more mature than that, Frankie."

I felt *awful*. I didn't know what was worse – being disappointed myself, or disappointing Mum and Dad because of the way I was reacting.

"Sorry," I mumbled, and went up to my room.

I felt kind of hopeless, you know? I mean, what was the point of getting all glammed up to go out, if we were going to be back home as soon as we got there? What made it worse was that Kenny wasn't even going to be there. She can always manage to cheer me up, however gloomy I am.

There was a knock at the door.

"Can I come in?" Mum peeped round the corner, then came in and sat on the bed.

"Sorry you're so disappointed, love, it's just that I'm kind of tired, you know." Mum did look a bit pale, and she still looked to be in pain from her indigestion. I suddenly felt very guilty for being so selfish.

"I'm sorry, Mum, I know you really aren't looking forward to going at all," I smiled apologetically. "And I guess I might be fed up of Fliss's 'Isn't-this-a-wonderful-party and isn't-my-mum-clever?' routine after two hours anyway!"

Mum just laughed. "OK then, you'd better get your glad rags on before your dad decides not to go at all!"

Then Mum noticed the fake tattoo I'd put round my arm. She stared at it, and I really thought she was going to go ballistic...

Then a big grin spread over her face.

"Is that one of the tattoos Lyndz gave you for Christmas?"

I nodded.

"Will you put that rose one on me, just there?" She pointed to her shoulder. "I can't wait to see Nikki's reaction when she sees it!"

We both collapsed into fits of giggles and went into the bathroom.

I have to say that Mum looked *well* cool when I'd finished with her. Not only did I apply the tattoo for her, but she also let me do her make-up. When we were both dressed, we went downstairs together and Dad whistled really loudly.

"Wowee!" he smirked. "You both look fantastic! You'd better wrap up warm though, it's starting to snow."

He hadn't even *noticed* Mum's tattoo! When she put on a jacket as we went outside, she gave me this big, soppy wink. We couldn't stop giggling all the way to the party, and Dad just couldn't work out what was going on.

"What is it with you two?" he asked. "You're like a couple of monkeys."

That, of course, made us laugh even more.

When we pulled up outside Fliss's house, there seemed to be loads of noise coming from inside.

"It sounds pretty lively!" Dad said.

And I suddenly began to feel really nervous. I knew that the others would be there and Mum and Dad and everything, but I really began to miss Kenny. We're always there to support each other, and I knew that she wouldn't be nervous about going into a big party at all.

We started to walk carefully up the path. The snow was starting to settle, and it was kind of slippery. I gingerly slid one foot in front of the other – and that's when I saw it. A figure. A very familiar figure. A figure wearing a bright Leicester City top. A figure which just *had* to be Kenny!

11

"Kenny!" I yelled, tottering up the path as fast as I dared. "What are you doing here?"

Kenny turned to me, beaming all over her face. "Blizzards and flu," she said, ever so seriously.

"You what?"

"There are going to be blizzards in Scotland and Granny and Grandpa have gone down with flu," Kenny explained. "So here we are!"

We grabbed each other and did one of our silly dances. Well Kenny did – she was wearing her trainers so she was all right in the snow. I just kind of stood there whilst she danced round me.

"You are so childish, do you know that?" moaned a voice from the shadows.

Uh-oh! If Kenny had made it to the party, then so had her cruddy sister, Molly the Monster.

"Molly's in a foul mood because Emma's at home with Stuart and Tom, and she wanted to stay too. But Mum said she was too young and had to come here with us, worse luck!" Kenny whispered.

"That doesn't mean she'll have to hang around with us, does it?" I asked anxiously.

"No fear!" huffed Kenny dismissively.

Mum and Dad meanwhile were walking up the path with Kenny's parents. They all get on pretty well together, so I was kind of hoping that Mum and Dad might stay at the party a bit longer now that they were here too.

Suddenly the front door opened and the music from inside the house spilled out to meet us.

"Oh good, it's you! Do come in and let me take

your coats," twittered Fliss's mum, staring very hard at our shoes. Now we all know how fussy she is about us trailing dirt into her house, so we all wiped our feet extra hard before we went in.

She was looking very thin and glamorous in a slinky evening dress, which was just like the one Fliss had worn to Lyndz's sleepover. She had a pinched look on her face and a strange sort of smile, as though she was trying to enjoy herself but hadn't quite cracked it.

"Felicity darling, help me with these, would you?" she called out.

And Fliss appeared, looking like an exact replica of her mum. But a lot younger, obviously. They had the same hairstyle and the same make-up, everything. They even had the same odd expression. It was really weird.

"Hello, let me take those," Fliss said ever so politely.

"Are you all right, Fliss? You look as though you need to go to the toilet or something," said Kenny, barging past her into the hall.

132

"Kenny!" reprimanded her mother, but she didn't sound very cross.

Mum and I took off our snow-covered jackets and gave them to Mrs Sidebotham. And, well – you should have been there to see the look on her face when she clocked our tattoos! For a few moments she just stared at my arm and Mum's shoulder. Then she huffed a bit, opening her mouth with no sound coming out. The she went really pink and hurriedly took our jackets into the cloakroom.

Dad looked kind of shocked when he noticed Mum's tattoo. Then he cracked up laughing and Mum had to push him into the lounge. As we were waiting for Andy to give us a drink he whispered, "You are two very wicked women!"

If Mum had known anything about high fives, we'd have done one then!

Lyndz was already there with her parents, so Kenny and I made a beeline for her.

"Have we missed anything?" I asked.

"Nah, only Fliss's mum going off on one because

133

someone had trailed muck on to the carpet."

"Nothing new there then," we all screeched together and spluttered into our Cokes.

"Ryan Scott's not here?" I asked when we'd recovered. "I was sure that Fliss would have invited him after he sent her that card."

"Don't get her started on that!" groaned Lyndz. "She's already told me twenty times how she wanted to invite him but her mum wouldn't let her."

Lyndz then turned to Kenny. "I didn't expect to see you here either."

Whilst Kenny was telling her all about the blizzards and the flu, I had a look round. Mum was sitting on the sofa deep in conversation with Lyndz's mum, talking about babies no doubt. Dad, Andy and Dr McKenzie were huddled together by the drinks cabinet. Callum was sitting under a table with a huge bowl of crisps, and Mrs McKenzie looked to be having words with a very sulky Molly. Fliss was nowhere to be seen. I went into the hall to investigate, and saw her wrestling with the front part of Adam's wheelchair, trying to get it up the front step. Rosie and her mum were behind, pushing, and Adam was beaming regally at everyone like a king.

"Here, let me help!" I rushed over to them.

After a few minutes of heaving, Adam was in.

"That was a close one, Adam!" I grinned. "We nearly had to bring the party out to you!"

He nodded and laughed and presented a bunch of flowers to Mrs Sidebotham, who was hovering anxiously behind the door.

"Thank you, that's very kind!" she said very slowly. People always seem to do that with Adam. Just because he has cerebral palsy and finds it difficult to speak himself, it doesn't mean he can't understand you.

Rosie wheeled him through to the lounge and everyone went to say hello.

"Fliss's mum's going to have a fit about that wheelchair!" whispered Lyndz. "You can't exactly wipe the wheels on the mat, can you?"

I had visions of Mrs Sidebotham flipping

completely. But she was being very brave and pretending not to notice the dirty, snowy tyre-marks that had criss-crossed over her cream carpet.

"Hey Rosie, come and join us!" we called over.

Kenny went to fetch her a glass of Coke and the rest of us chatted together. But after about ten minutes there was still no sign of Kenny. I went into the kitchen to look for her, and found Mum tucking into some garlic bread.

"I thought you had indigestion," I said.

"It's not too bad at the moment," she told me. "Besides, I've got to keep my strength up. I'm eating for two, remember?"

"Yeah, right!" I laughed. "Well make sure you leave some food for us, OK!"

I still couldn't see Kenny anywhere. But I could hear raised voices coming from the downstairs loo.

"I never wanted to come to this downbeat party anyway. We'd be having much more fun in Scotland."

"Yeah, well we're not in Scotland, are we, so you'd better start livening up before you depress everybody else, you miserable toad!"

That had to be Kenny and Molly doing their usual sweet sister act.

"Hey guys, come on. Give it a rest, for goodness' sake!" I burst in on them. It's a good thing I did too, because Kenny had Molly pinned up against the wall.

I broke them up and they reluctantly followed me back into the kitchen, where Kenny quickly swooped on the food.

"Grub! Great, I'm starving!"

She started piling things on to a plate.

"No wonder you're getting fat, eating like that!" Molly sneered.

"Right, that's it!"

Kenny grabbed a spoon and loaded it with sour cream dip. She took aim, and was about to fire it when…

"Hey not so fast!" Andy grabbed her arm and took away the spoon. "We'll have no food fights

137

here, thank you very much. That would definitely finish Nikki off!"

Molly started laughing mockingly at Kenny, who looked absolutely furious.

"What about taking some food in to Adam, Molly?" Andy suggested. "And I thought you two might like to help Fliss and Lyndz sort out the music for dancing. It's about time this party got going. What do you say?"

"Cool!" We piled in to the lounge.

All the adults seemed to be standing around talking, but I couldn't see Mum anywhere.

"She's around somewhere," Dad told me. "I've just seen her with a plate full of cheesecake!"

We both laughed and I went to join the others, who were sorting through a stack of CDs.

When we'd got everything sorted, we put the finishing touches to one of our Sugababes routines. Fliss was wiggling for all she was worth when her mum appeared and started flapping her arms about too. I kind of assumed that she was trying to join in, until I heard her squeaking:

"Can everyone be quiet for a minute?"

But of course nobody heard her. So she tried again. But still everyone carried on chatting.

"Would you like me to get everyone's attention?" asked Kenny.

"Thank you, Kenny, that would be very kind," she smiled.

Kenny stood on a chair, put two fingers in her mouth and made the most ear-splitting whistle ever. Then she yelled:

"LISTEN UP EVERYBODY, MRS SIDEBOTHAM WANTS TO SAY SOMETHING!"

Well, that certainly shut everyone up.

"Er thanks, Kenny, that's not exactly what I had in mind!" Mrs Sidebotham said lamely, and everyone laughed. "I'd just like to say, er – where's Andy?"

"Is that it?" asked Kenny. "I thought it was something important!"

Everybody screamed with laughter, but Fliss's mum seemed quite anxious to find him. So we all looked round, and then we heard the downstairs toilet flush. We heard a running of water and whistling, and Andy reappeared in the lounge to great guffaws and a huge round of applause. Fliss's mum looked dead embarrassed, but Andy just smirked.

Fliss's mum tried again.

"As you know, Andy and I…"

"Erm, sorry to interrupt you, Nikki…"

It was Dad. I couldn't believe it! Fliss's mum was starting to look really annoyed.

"If you're going to make an important announcement, I'd really like Helena to hear it, and I don't think she's here."

Everyone looked round again. Mum was definitely not there. Where on earth was she?

12

Now I don't know if you've seen my mum since she's been pregnant, but she is kind of big. She's usually just normal-sized, but expecting the baby had made her balloon into a big, fat, waddly duck. And to be honest, I was worried that she'd got stuck somewhere.

When we'd all done a thorough search downstairs, Dad whispered that maybe I should check upstairs too.

"You know what she's like when she's had a

plateful of cheesecake – BAM – she's out like a light. Just check that she hasn't crashed out on one of the beds," he suggested.

"Like Goldilocks, you mean!" I laughed.

"Yeah, something like that!"

I crept upstairs and tried all the bedrooms. First Fliss's, which was as neat as usual. I looked at her bed, but there was only a row of dolls looking back at me. I peeped inside her mum's bedroom too, but I felt kind of guilty doing that. I know how Mrs Sidebotham hates anyone going in there without her permission. It smelt all perfumed and lovely, like roses.

"Mum? Are you here?" I hissed.

There was no reply, and I could see from the doorway that the only things on the bed were a few frilly cushions.

Next there was Callum's room. I'd never been in there before. It smelt all funny, like little boys tend to do. And it was kind of hard to see where anything was. I crept in a little bit further and BANG – I stumbled into something. Then there was a groan.

"Mum!" I squeaked. "Is that you?"

I fumbled for the light switch and flicked it on.

"Whaddyawant?" a small, weary voice murmured. It was Callum, lying on the bed and shielding his eyes from the light.

"Nothing," I whispered. "Sorry to disturb you, go back to sleep!"

I switched off the light and went back on to the landing. There were only two places left to try – the room where Fliss's mum practises her beauty therapy and the bathroom. I figured Mum might have gone to lie down on Mrs Sidebotham's treatment couch. So I was going to try there first, when I heard a noise coming from the bathroom.

"Mum, is that you?" I called out, my face right up to the door.

"Frankie?"

"Are you OK? We were worried about you? Fliss's mum is making an announcement and Dad thought you ought to come down," I told her.

143

"Actually, Frankie, do you think you could get your dad for me?" Mum called back.

"You haven't got indigestion again, have you?" I asked. "Dad told me about you eating that cheesecake…"

"No!" she interrupted me, gasping slightly. "I'm sure… the baby's… on its way… this time."

"Hold on Mum! I'll get Dad!" I shouted, and flew downstairs like a mad woman.

"Dad, Dad, quick! Mum says she's having the baby!"

Suddenly everyone seemed to be rushing around like headless chickens.

"Call an ambulance, will you Nikki?" Dad shouted, leaping up the stairs two at a time.

Lyndz's mum hurried after him. She'd been teaching Mum's ante-natal classes, so she was kind of a good person to have around. And then of course there was Kenny's dad, who's a doctor.

"I'll go and get my bag from the car!" He opened the front door and was met by a blizzard of snow. "My goodness me! I thought

144

it was supposed to be Scotland that was going to get all the bad weather," he said, stumbling out into the cold.

I felt really strange, like everything was going on around me but I wasn't part of it.

"Dad, Dad! Can I help?" Kenny rushed over to her father as soon as he came back through the door.

"I'm not sure that Helena would thank me for giving her an inexperienced, under-age midwife!" Dr McKenzie laughed, ruffling Kenny's hair. Then he noticed how disappointed she looked. "But there are lots of important things you can do. Like getting a bed ready for her to lie down on until the ambulance arrives."

"My bed!" whimpered Fliss's mum as Kenny hared upstairs. "My beautiful bedroom!"

Peeping up through the banisters, I could see Dad and Mrs Collins helping Mum into the bedroom. Mum caught sight of me.

"Don't look so worried, Frankie, I'm fine." She tried to smile, despite wincing with pain. "And look at all this attention I'm getting. It's better than hospital!"

Yeah, right! Like every woman would choose to give birth in Fliss's home on New Year's Eve!

"Your mum's right." Lyndz's dad gently led me into the lounge where everyone else was sitting around anxiously. "What Lyndz's mum doesn't know about giving birth you can write on the back of a stamp!"

"I had all my children at home," Mrs McKenzie told me reassuringly. "And Kenny's father assisted at all the births. So your mum really is in good hands. Come on over by the fire, love, you're cold. Fliss, can you rustle up a warm drink for Frankie? I think she's in a bit of shock."

Fliss was looking very pale and in a state of shock herself, but she went into the kitchen and Rosie and Lyndz came over to join me.

"We're not going to forget this party in a hurry, are we?" squeaked Rosie. "And just think, we're all going to be here when your baby brother or sister is born! How cool is that?"

"I think labour sometimes takes quite a while,"

Lyndz told us. "The ambulance will probably be here soon, and then they'll take your mum to hospital."

Kenny bounded in, all flushed and excited.

"Dad says we might need some towels, is that all right, Mrs S?"

Fliss's mum shuddered slightly and nodded.

"It's like being in one of those old movies, isn't it?" said Rosie's mum. "You know, they always say 'I'll need lots of towels and plenty of hot water' whenever anyone's about to give birth."

Kenny stopped in the doorway and spun round. "Hey, that's an idea! What about Frankie's mum having the baby in your Jacuzzi bath, Mrs S? A water birth would be so cool!"

"Oh no!" Fliss's mum started sobbing. "I… I… don't think so!"

She seemed to be kind of gasping a bit, so Mrs McKenzie shooed Kenny back upstairs and poured a brandy.

"For the shock!" she murmured, handing it to Fliss's mum.

Rosie's mum had been spluttering with laughter ever since Kenny mentioned her great idea about the Jacuzzi, and she was laughing even harder at the thought of Mrs Sidebotham having to be revived by brandy.

A few minutes later, Andy and Fliss appeared with a big tray of drinks and biscuits for everyone. They both seemed very concerned that Mrs Sidebotham was in such a state. I mean, excuse me, but wasn't it *my* mum who was upstairs having a baby?

"How long did the ambulance say they would be, Nikki?" Dr McKenzie called downstairs.

Fliss's mum leapt up and yelped, like she'd just sat on a wasp or something.

"Oh no, I didn't, I mean… I thought… oh dear!"

We all stared at her.

"You mean, you never even called an ambulance?" Andy asked her sharply.

"No!" she whispered, and started to cry again.

"I'll do it!" he sighed and went into the hall.

"I thought this party was really lame, but it's

kind of getting exciting now!" Molly chuckled as she walked past us with a piece of cake stuffed in her mouth.

I would normally have said something, but I couldn't. I was more worried about Mum. I mean, like Gran had said, she wasn't all that young to be having a baby. And to be having it in someone else's house, with no ambulance and a blizzard outside – well, it looked pretty bad.

I wanted to find out what was happening but I couldn't. I tried to stand up, but my legs had turned to jelly and I fell back down again.

"There there, my love!" Kenny's mum helped me to sit down again. And to my horror, I started to cry.

"Will Mum be OK?" I whispered through my sobs.

"I'll go to find out, you just stay here," she told me kindly.

Rosie's mum came over to sit by me and Adam wheeled himself over. He looked so sad, it made me want to cry all over again. Rosie and Lyndz came to sit by me too, and so did Fliss.

"It'll be all right, Mum's bedroom's ever so clean," she said reassuringly, stroking my arm. "I mean, Mum cleans so much, it's probably even cleaner than the hospital!"

What is she like? It did make us all laugh though, and then Fliss was dead pleased and pretended that she'd said it on purpose.

"They said that everything's a bit delayed because of the snow," Andy told us as he came back into the lounge. "But an ambulance will be here as soon as possible. Hey, what's the rush?"

Kenny had hurtled downstairs and right into him.

"It's so cool, Frankie, your mum's doing great, she's going 'whoo, whoo, hee'…" She started puffing and blowing and making all these weird sounds.

"You haven't been watching, have you?" Lyndz sounded really shocked.

"Course not!" said Kenny indignantly. "But I've been doing stuff for Dad, and I can hear from the landing. Come on, Frankie, you should come too!"

She dragged me to my feet. But when we got

to the bottom of the steps, I heard the most amazing sound. A baby was crying. I could hear Mum laughing and Dad cooing, "Welcome to the world, little one!" And all the time, there was this newborn crying.

I can't describe how I felt. I was really *really* happy, but I just stood there with tears streaming down my face.

"Congratulations!" The others all rushed over to hug me.

"Hey, Frankie!" Dad appeared at the top of the steps. "You'd better come and say hello to your little sister!"

I had a sister! My very own little sister!

I don't know how I got upstairs, my legs were still so wobbly. But just as I got to the landing, I heard chiming. Someone must have turned on the television because that was definitely the sound of Big Ben. I was really confused. I was sure only an hour had passed since we found out about Mum, but it must have been more like three.

"Come on everyone, it's almost midnight!" someone shouted.

I couldn't believe it. It was almost New Year!

13

BONG!

I rushed into the bedroom.

"Mum! Dad! Oh wow!" My little sister was all tiny and bewildered and snuggled up in a towel. She was so beautiful.

BONG!

There was a lot of noise on the landing.

BONG!

"Here we are, guys!" Andy brought in a tray of champagne glasses. He'd even got one for me with a tiny bit of real champagne in the bottom of it. He winked at me.

"If you can't celebrate the birth of your own sister, I don't know what you can celebrate!" he laughed.

I peeped round the bedroom door, and everyone was standing up the stairs and on the landing.

"We thought we should all be together!" Kenny whispered to me. My eyes started filling with tears again. I couldn't ever remember feeling so happy.

BONG!

I'd lost count of the bongs, but that must have been the last one because everybody started hugging each other. Dr McKenzie started singing that song 'Auld Lang Syne' and everybody joined in. They all held hands, even though some of them were on the stairs.

"We should have taught you the words after all!" Mum grinned at me from the bed. She looked kind of hot and sleepy.

"All we need now is a tall dark stranger to let in

the New Year!" chirped Fliss's mum, who seemed to have perked up again.

And you're not going to believe this, but just then the doorbell rang. We all peered over the banisters to get a better view, but all we could hear was Fliss's mum giggling, "Well you're not quite what I expected. But you'll do!"

We all cracked up when she led in a paramedic in his fluorescent green jacket. "I don't suppose you've got a piece of coal and a bottle of whisky in that bag, have you?" shouted Andy.

"Fraid not!" he laughed. "Are my patients up here?"

Mrs Sidebotham led him upstairs through the crowd of people, and another paramedic appeared, wheeling in a stretcher. It was only then it started to sink in. *My mum had just had a baby!*

I was still all covered in goosebumps when the paramedics started to carry Mum downstairs on the stretcher. Everybody scooted down into the hall to make way for them.

"Mother and baby are both doing well," Dad announced proudly. "Thanks to Patsy and Jim here!"

Everybody applauded Lyndz's mum and Kenny's dad. They both looked dead embarrassed.

"I'm going to go to hospital with Helena," Dad told me as he stroked Mum's beaming face.

"And you're going to come home with us, Frankie," said Kenny's mum, smiling at me.

"All *right*!" yelled Kenny, to everyone's amusement.

"But before we go, Nikki," Dad said, "what was that announcement you were trying to make? Before my wife so rudely interrupted you!"

Everyone turned to look at Fliss's mum, who had gone bright pink.

"Erm, well, erm…"

"We're finally taking the plunge and getting married," Andy announced for her.

"Thank you, Andy!" Mrs Sidebotham looked a bit miffed at him for taking away her moment of glory like that. But as soon as everyone started cheering and shouting "Congratulations!" she soon cheered up. In fact, she was soon beaming so much, I thought her face might split. And Fliss looked dead chuffed too.

"We ought to say congratulations to Helena and Gwyn as well," Andy shouted when the noise had died down a little. "Here's to the little one!"

The paramedics seemed kind of keen to get Mum into the ambulance, so I kissed them again and waved to them from the front door. Then I went back inside.

What an evening it had been! I looked at Fliss's mum, and I couldn't help feeling a tiny bit sorry for her. She'd arranged this whole party to announce her engagement and Mum had sort of hijacked it. Still, Mrs Sidebotham had loads of attention now. All the women were cooing over her and asking about the wedding arrangements. And Fliss was in the thick of it, talking about dresses and flowers. Anybody would think it was *her* wedding they were planning! Still, at least I knew now what she'd meant about one of her wishes coming true in the New Year!

"Come on, Frankie! Let's party!" Kenny

dragged me into the lounge where Andy had put on Justin Timberlake.

I was kind of tired, but it was a *great* night. I mean, that morning I'd expected to be home by ten o'clock. And there I was bopping away at almost one o'clock in the morning! It was as wild as one of our sleepovers!

About half an hour later though, I could feel my energy running out like a battery. I wasn't the only one. Everyone else seemed to be pretty exhausted too. As we left, the only ones still dancing were Fliss's mum and Andy. And I'd been wrong about her – she was a pretty nifty mover!

Of course, going home with Kenny was great, even if it did mean having to listen to Molly the Monster moaning. According to her, it had been the worst party in the world, full of sad old people.

"Ignore her," Kenny whispered. "She's only mad because there weren't any boys there. I thought it was the coolest party ever!"

I grinned. It *had* been pretty amazing.

I crashed out as soon as I got to Kenny's. I slept

on the floor between Kenny and Molly's beds. Molly nearly freaked because she hadn't had a chance to hide all her things like she does before our sleepovers. But I was too exhausted to look at any of her things anyway. In fact I didn't wake up until about nine o'clock, and only then because Kenny's mum was calling me, saying that Dad was there.

It was great to see him. And even better when he took me straight to hospital to see Mum and my baby sister. It was just so cool, sitting there holding this tiny thing who was my new sister. I couldn't really get my head round it, it felt so weird. Weird in a very nice way, though.

Mum was only in hospital for a couple of days. I think she'd been kind of worried that they'd keep the baby in because she was born early. But the doctors said that she was doing really well, so she came home too. I'd made a big banner saying:

Welcome home Mum and ...

But Mum and Dad hadn't agreed on a name

yet, so I just drew a slightly wonky baby instead. I hung it in the hall so it was the first thing they saw. I loved carrying my sister round and showing her everything. Mum said that she was too young to focus on anything properly, but I knew that she was taking it all in.

Best of all was introducing her to my sleepover friends. They all cooed over her and went completely mushy. Even Kenny, but don't tell her I told you so! Fliss of course is too full of her mum's wedding plans to think about anything else. And she has this romantic idea of inviting Ryan Scott as her guest.

"Get real, Fliss!" hooted Kenny. "Guys hate mushy stuff. That will put him off you for life!"

"Besides, your mum's wedding is ages away," Rosie reminded her. "We've got loads of other stuff to do before then."

"Yeah. Like destroying the M&Ms for a start!" Kenny reminded us. "I bet they're still mad with us about all that Christmas play stuff."

"We ought to get a plan together," suggested

Lyndz. "You know, just so we're ready for them when they do something awful to us."

"Yeah, let's do something really gross!" I suggested. "It was one of our New Year's resolutions, after all!"

So that's what we're meeting up to do now. The others have probably hatched a plan already, seeing as I'm so late. I keep telling them that it's worth it. I'm only late because I have to help out with my baby sister and she is sort of a new member of the Sleepover Club after all!

Oh no! Did you hear a scream? Either Kenny's acting out a wicked plan for the M&Ms, or she's strangling Fliss because she's sick of her going on about the wedding! I'd better go and sort them out. Come on, before it's too late!

Here are the Sleepover Clubber's all-time fave party games. Have fun with these, or make up your own

Lyndz

The **obstacle race** for me – I can set up jumps and pretend I'm on a horse!

Fliss

I'll have a go at the **three-legged race**, but only if we use a pink scarf to tie our legs together.

Kenny

Fliss! Only you would want to look that stylish! Let's have a **tug of war**!

Rosie

Good luck getting anyone to play tug of war in their party gear, Kenny. How about **pass the balloon** – let's see if you can do it without using your hands.

Frankie

Guys! Let's just have a bop and eat lots of crisps! If you don't want to play my fave game – **Let's tickle Lyndz till she hiccups** – check out what other fab things you can do to make your party go with a bang…

Fliss's fruity ice cubes

1. Get a selection of fruit: raspberries, cut strawberries, blueberries
2. Put one piece of fruit in each section of an ice-cube tray
3. Fill the ice-cube tray with water and freeze (or try freezing fruit juice)
4. When frozen, pop some ice cubes in a jug of lemonade and watch the fruit appear as the cubes melt. Yummy!

I might get the others to eat some fruit this way! So good for the complexion.

Fliss ✗

Get partying, whatever time of year!

The Look

Spring party

fresh and bright:
cut spring flowers, try
daffodils and tulips

Summer party

laid-back lounging:
deck chairs and sun
umbrellas and lanterns

Autumn party

cosy and chilled-out:
rugs on the sofa,
hollowed-out pumpkins

Winter party

Christmas grotto:
paper chains, baubles,
anything glittery

New Year party tip

Can't make it till midnight? If you're having a New Year party, why not celebrate the Australian New Year – they're eleven hours ahead of the UK so you can party at lunch time!

Food and Drink

mini chocolate eggs

hot-cross buns

icy lemonade

ice cream

fruit smoothies

iced fairy cakes

toffee apples

pumpkin soup

flapjacks

hot sausage rolls

hot chocolate

marshmallows

What to Wear

fab accessories:

multicoloured hair

slides and silver bangles

something floaty:

mini or maxi dresses

with cute sandals

something different:

boots with a dress

and patterned tights

something warm!

jeans and slim-fitting

shirt

Rosie x   Kenny x

Fliss x   Lyndz x   Frankie x

It's time to get on the dance floor with Frankie's top boogie tracks

Something from the eighties

80's

Waiting for a Star to Fall.....................................Boy Meets Girl

I Should Be So Lucky..Kylie Minogue

Wake Me Up Before you Go-Go...............................Wham!

Girls on Film..Duran Duran

Something from the nineties

90's

Girls Just Wanna Have Fun.................................Cindi Lauper

Let Me Entertain You...Robbie Williams

Chain Reaction..Diana Ross

Livin' La Vida Loca...Ricky Martin

Vogue...Madonna

Something from the noughties
(that's 2000 and beyond!)

00's

Mercy	Duffy
Dancing Queen	Meryl Streep
Put a Ring on It	Beyonce
Womanizer	Britney Spears
Umbrella	Rhianna

Why don't you put together your own fave tracks?
Remember, whatever kind of party you're having,
turn it up loud and dance to the sound! We'll catch
you at the next Sleepover.

Frankie x

Rosie's decorated party notebook

You will need:

- An old notepad or notebook
- Lots of glitter, stickers, coloured pens, pieces of fabric, pictures cut out of magazines
- Glue

1. Decorate the front of your notebook by covering it with the fabric or by sticking a blank piece of paper on it. Then get busy and personalise it with the stickers, pens, pictures, glitter and glue.

2. If you're going to have the best party ever, why not record it? Write the date of each party in the book and record what you were wearing, or stick photos of you and your friends in it.

Rosie x

You are invited to join Frankie, Lyndz, Fliss, Kenny and me for a groovy sleepover in...

Dance-Off!

The Sleepover Babes are on a mission to win the school dance competition - no way are we letting our enemies, the M&Ms, dance all over us!

Have **you** got some funky moves? Come along and join the club!

From

Rosie x

You are invited to join Frankie, Lyndz, Fliss, Rosie and me on our next crazy adventure in...

The Sleepover Club

Hit the Beach!

I L.O.V.E. sports and am soooo excited about our school trip. A week away from home with my best friends by the seaside - time to catch some waves!

Are **you** up for some fun in the sun? Grab your shades and join the club!

From

Kenny x

You are invited to join Frankie, Lyndz, Rosie, Fliss and me for our next sleepover in...

The **SleePover Club**

Trick or Treat

It's Halloween, and we were going to have the best sleepover ever, but my big sis Molly has ruined everything! I think it's time for some spooktastic revenge...

Hop on **your** broomstick and

Join the club!

From

Kenny x

YOU are invited to join Frankie, Lyndz, Kenny, Fliss and me for our next sleepover in...

The SleePover Club
WITHDRAWN

Star Girls

Frankie's Mad Uncle Colin gave her a telescope for her birthday, and now the Sleepover Club have gone star-gazing mad! Who knows we might even spot a UFO...

Are **YOU** ready to see stars?

Then come along and join the club!

From

Rosie x